Watched

Suddenly, Lori got the feeling that she was being watched. Not in the way that someone watches a band perform, but *stared at*. She scanned the big room . . .

There. In the back.

Blake Cutler stood along the far wall of the gym, wearing his letterman jacket over a polo shirt. His football buddies stood next to him, exuding an arrogance particular to all jocks that Lori had come to despise. Blake was many things: a star quarterback, one of the top five cutest guys at Roosevelt High, and Lori's angry, jealous ex who blamed her for the end of their relationship.

Blake Cutler was glaring at her, unblinking, with the most fiery anger she'd ever seen.

He looked like he wanted to kill her.

Other Terrorcore Rewind paperbacks you will enjoy:

Baby's Breath
by A.D. Aro

The Hushed Boys
by Caleb J. Pecue

The Stuffing
by Austin Hinderliter

The Magician
by Vanessa Leonardo

G.D. Bowlin

No part of this publication may be reproduced in whole or in part, or stored in a retrieval system, or transmitted in any form or by any means, electronic, mechanical, photocopying, recording, or otherwise, without written permission of the publisher. For information regarding permission, write to Terrorcore Publishing LLC, 119 Homestead Ct., Edwardsville, Illinois 62025.

ISBN 979-8-9889138-9-4

Copyright © 2026 by G.D. Bowlin. All rights reserved. Published by Terrorcore Publishing LLC. REWIND is a retro-inspired line of nostalgic horror YA books. These books are suitable for kids thirteen or older. For more information regarding content, please email terrorcorepublishing@gmail.com or visit our website at: www.terrorcorepublishing.com/contact.

12 11 10 9 8 7 6 5 4 3 2 1 0

Cover art by Creepy Carves Design.

Printed in the U.S.A.

First Terrorcore printing, March 2026

*For Jimmy Champane,
the biggest horror fan I know.*

Chapter 1

Being on stage frightened Lori, but that only made her want to do it more. She lived by the philosophy that if you weren't doing something that scared you, you were doing it wrong.

That was a good thing too, she thought as she looked around the cavernous, shadowy backstage area. Not only was the place creepy with its dark corners and heavy, old, red velvet curtains, it was a safety hazard. Electrical sockets that sparked when an amp was plugged in, weak spots in the stage that could give out under sneakers.

She tuned all that out and focused on the satisfying weight of the electric guitar hanging off her shoulder.

Lori loved the way the vintage Fender Jaguar felt in her hands. It had been her dad's when he was alive. Now, it was hers. The silken feel of the maple neck, worn smooth from years of playing. She knew how every note sang out as her fingers danced along the frets. No matter how hard life got, when she was on stage with his old guitar, she was at peace.

She gripped the neck of the instrument with both hands and closed her eyes. Through its wood she felt the power of the music, the power of all the time she and her father had spent working on it together. They had meant to name it, but had never gotten around to it. Now, she couldn't seem to settle on anything, unable to receive his input.

She took long, deep breaths, working to center herself before going on stage.

The other members of Lori's band, Crying Lilacs, thought this meditative prayer thing was totally weird. She understood why, but she didn't care. Everyone had rituals before a show, and this was what she needed to do backstage before the curtain rose.

"Earth to Lori . . ." Seth's voice pulled Lori out of her reverie. "You're a space cadet sometimes."

She looked up to where Seth sat tuning his Gibson Les Paul Junior. A stripped-down, lean, mean machine.

"I'm getting in the zone, dude," she said back, hoping she didn't sound defensive.

The truth was, Seth made her feel a little nervous sometimes—well, maybe nervous wasn't the right word. It was more like an edgy kind of excitement. Butterflies in her stomach.

Yes, Seth was cute. She hated to admit it, because he wasn't her usual type at all. Before he'd joined the band, he'd been clean cut, but now he was growing his hair out to look more like their heroes: Kurt Cobain, Eddie Vedder, Mark Lanegan. Now, his jet-black hair was in an awkward in-between stage that marked him as the worst thing you could be in a grunge band—a poser.

Posers could have nice smiles and strong jawlines and sparkling blue eyes, too, though, Lori had learned.

She shut Seth out of her mind. No matter how cute she thought he was, it didn't matter. You never coupled up in a band. It destroyed groups from the inside, every time. Just look at Fleetwood Mac. Total career suicide. Crying Lilacs was the most important thing in the world to Lori. The one good thing that might pave the way to a future for her, and Seth was already proving to be a hugely talented, integral part of their sound.

She reminded herself to think with her head, not her hormones.

"Earth to Seth," Meadow said from where she was sitting on the top of her bass amp, which was nearly as tall as she was. Her voice dripped with sarcasm, which wasn't unusual, especially when she was talking to Seth. "You need to get some better jokes. They call that a cliché."

"Whatever," Seth said and went back to tuning his guitar.

Meadow gave Lori a wicked little grin. Lori knew that Meadow didn't care for Seth. She smelled poser all over him and was quick to remind Lori that he'd never approached them to jam until Crying Lilacs had started booking shows and become popular, at least in their little rural North Carolinian town of Red Elm. She wasn't wrong. Seth had only talked his way into the band after they'd played pretty much every small venue that would allow high schoolers onstage.

If it had been up to Meadow, Seth wouldn't even have been in the band, but Lori was the founder, songwriter, and de facto leader of Crying Lilacs. She listened to everyone, but at the end of the day, she called the shots.

Lori heard her drummer, Memphis, before she saw him. His big feet clomped from the recesses backstage until he emerged from the shadows. He carried the kick drum from his kit like it was nothing. At six foot three, he would have been imposing if his aura weren't so gentle.

He set the drum down, brushed away the long, messy hair that was always hanging in his face, and said, "That's everything for me. Just gotta like, get everything set up, you know?"

Meadow stuck her hand out, and Memphis automatically high-fived her. The two of them had been best friends since, well, as long as Lori could remember. Fourth grade at least. They were inseparable. As the Crying Lilacs rhythm section, they read each other's instincts and anticipated each other's changes. She couldn't have asked for better bandmates or, more importantly, friends.

"How's your nerves, Bigfoot?" Meadow asked Memphis.

"My guts are going nuts. You think JoEllen's gonna be out there? She's so pretty, man. If I mess up in front of her, like, there's no coming back from that. I'm dead, dude. I swear, I'm dead."

"Okay, okay." Meadow reached into the shaggy halo of hair that hung around her heart-shaped face. Her golden yellow roots were well past showing through an electric blue dye-job. She came back out of the snarled curls with a thick, tightly rolled joint that she had tucked behind her ear. "Hey boss, you mind if we go under the stage and *uh*, get in the zone too?"

"*Oh, uh*, I gotta get my kit set up," Memphis said.

Lori smiled at him. "It's all right. I know how you like your hi-hat placed. Do what you gotta do. But do it in ten? The curtain's up in fifteen."

Meadow gave Lori a little wink. She hopped down from the amp and led Memphis back into the shadows.

"They're gonna do that *here*?" Seth's voice had an edge of worry to it. "They're gonna get caught."

Poser, thought Lori for a fleeting moment.

"There's a little trapdoor that leads under the stage." Lori looked up from her guitar to give Seth a reassuring smile. "We found it accidentally when we first played here last year."

Lori set her Jaguar down into its stand. She moved over to Memphis' battered drum kit and began to move the pieces around.

"Hey, let me help you with that," Seth offered.

Lori shook her head. "I got it. I've done this a million times."

She centered the kick drum and tested the action of the pedal. *Pop, pop, pop*. The sound always sent a jolt of excitement through her.

"I was thinking...*um*, when we play 'Born Tonight, Die Tomorrow,' that I might put a little something over the bridge."

Whenever Seth came to Lori with a new musical idea, he did it with a nervous energy, like a kitten bringing their owner a bird they'd killed. It was cute. He shared his ideas as offerings that she, as leader, could refuse if she wanted—although she rarely did as they were usually pretty good.

"A little something?" she asked as she set up Memphis' hi-hat next to his snare drum. "What's that mean exactly?"

"Just a little lick I've been playing around with. It kinda goes like, *um, wha-wha-wha-woooo-widdle-whaaaa—*"

"Okay, okay," Lori said, laughing at his guitar impression. "I trust you. Go for it."

"Thanks! You know, I noticed that Meadow and Memphis smoke before every show."

"It's not a big deal. Honestly, Memphis gets real bad stage fright. It helps him get over it and get behind the drums. Meadow just likes to party. But between you and me, I don't think she'd do it if it weren't for Memphis. They're attached at the hip. She doesn't want him to feel weird."

"I also noticed that you don't smoke at all," Seth said gently, careful to not pry. Then clarified, "Weed, anyway."

"I do sometimes... Every once in a while, at a party or something. I like to be clear-headed on stage. I wanna feel the notes, feel the energy from the audience. Maybe it's a control thing, but our songs mean everything to me. I want it all to be perfect. Sounds kinda psycho, I guess."

Seth gave her a warm, appreciative smile. "No, not at all. *Perfect*... that sounds nice. I'll do my best."

The two of them shared a laugh.

"You don't smoke either," Lori said.

"I just don't like drugs, I guess. Never tried them, never want to."

The statement hung in the air as Lori continued to work on the drums. She was actually glad to have someone in the band who was so responsible. But opinions like that made Seth sound like a cop or, worse, a dad.

"I know Meadow and Memphis think I'm a nerd," he said.

At least he's self-aware, Lori thought.

"Whatever, man," she said. "You're super talented. You can play like crazy. Who cares whether you get high or not?" Lori looked up from tightening the nut on a drum stand just long enough to see Seth blush a bit.

He walked across the creaking old stage and stopped on the other side of the drum kit, watching as Lori set up Memphis' crash cymbal. He still had that same slightly nervous energy, those big, brown puppy dog eyes.

"Lori, I just want to say thank you for giving me a shot in Crying Lilacs. Everyone knows you guys are the best band in town, and it's a big deal to be here. I get that, you know, and—*Oh, shoot!*"

Lori looked up, confused and a little annoyed. She wanted to hear more about how great her band was. Seth hurried back to his guitar setup on the right side of the stage. He darted around, searching for something.

"My fuzz pedal! I left it in the van. I knew I'd forgotten something. It just came to me. I gotta go, Lori, I'll be back in five seconds, I swear!"

Lori nodded and watched him hustle away backstage. She had no doubt he'd be back in time.

She finished setting up Memphis' tom drum. The

last piece of the puzzle was in place. She stepped back to admire her work.

Nice.

She looked out over the stage and took a deep breath, grateful for the moment before the show started. She could hear voices murmuring beyond the heavy velvet curtains. They were ready for Crying Lilacs. The Lilacs would be ready for them.

For a second, she thought she could hear Blake's voice out there, cutting above the crowd.

Oh God, please don't let Blake ruin tonight.

She caught a sudden chill and wrapped her arms around herself. Was it the thought of her abusive ex-boyfriend or the creepy backstage area that made her whole body feel like a freezer-burned Push Pop?

She was at the back of the sagging stage, close to the moldering old curtains that hung back there to cover up the inner workings of the mechanics: sandbags, levers and pulleys, ropes. The back curtains were even older than the ones hanging in the front. They smelled like what Lori imagined the inside of a rotting coffin would smell like, and she gagged a bit.

Shaking off the creepy feeling, she closed her eyes and worked to find her focus again.

She was almost there when a pair of rough, muscular hands gripped her around the shoulders and pulled her into the shadows.

Chapter 2

Blake. It had to be.

That icy feeling shot through Lori's veins again, and she froze as the big, callused hands spun her roughly around. She had instinctively closed her eyes. She forced them open and looked up into the threatening face of . . . Coach Teller.

Roosevelt High's tall, muscular P.E. teacher glowered down at her. His face was tan and creased from years spent out in the sun coaching the school's all-star track-and-field program. His tightly shorn, graying buzzcut made the top of his head look like a perfect square. He smelled like sunscreen and cigarettes.

Lori pulled away, wriggling out of the strong hands that were still gripped around her shoulders. She stepped away from him, out of arm's reach.

"C-Coach Teller, jeez," Lori gulped, nervously. "You scared me."

"Good. Maybe one of these days I'll scare you straight." Coach Teller's voice was low and gravelly. Threatening.

"I don't understand what you mean." Lori's initial shock was wearing off, and her fear was turning into anger. Who did he think he was, grabbing her like that? Scaring her?

"Sensimilla. Giggle smoke. *Goof butts.*" He hit each word harder, quickly building to the beginnings of what Lori knew would be a powerful lecture. About what, though, she wasn't sure.

"Goof butts? What are you talking about?"

"Marijuana, young lady! I can smell it back here, and I *know* you and your little band are back here 'toking up,' as they say. Disgraceful, disgusting conduct anywhere... But on school property? Over the line!"

School property. The comment was an aggressive reminder for Lori that Crying Lilacs weren't playing a proper venue. They were about to get on stage to perform at Roosevelt High's Spring Fling. The people on the other side of the curtain were her classmates.

Lori assumed the same formidable posture that Teller himself was always affecting around school: hands on hips, shoulders up, chest puffed out. If he wanted to get in her face, she would meet him at his own level.

"Listen, dude, I don't know what you're talking about. My band members had to run out to grab some equipment, and I'm all alone. As you can see, no pot on me." Her point, though dishonest, was well made. She had nothing on her, so he had nothing on her.

Lori figured he probably didn't know about the trapdoor. When they'd found it, it had been covered in what looked like half a century's worth of cobwebs. Unfortunately, Coach Teller was already revved up. There was no stopping him now.

"I've seen what's happening to these grunge bands. Druggies, burnouts. Ruining their lives. Their instruments are barely in tune! Even these bands started by girls like you. L7, Babes in Toyland, *Hole* . . . *ugh* . . . I don't even want to know what that name is in reference to. They're all a bunch of burnouts!" Coach Teller was red-faced now, neck vein throbbing, eyes bulging.

"You really know a lot of bands," Lori started and then added, "I'm actually impressed."

"No backchatter, Lori! You know, it's even worse that all these kids are giving Seattle such a bad name. The Pacific Northwest is one of America's finest landscapes. Untouched, unspoiled. It's God's country, Lori. You and your grungy little cohorts are micturating all over God's country."

"Look," Lori said. "I don't have time for this. We're on in five. You're not a cop. You probably shouldn't even be back here. I haven't done anything wrong, and I'm not holding. We both know you can't do anything. So, thanks for the advice or whatever, but I need to get ready to play."

For a long moment, Coach Teller sized her up with glaring, narrowed eyes. She stared right back, and he took a step forward. She backed up and was immediately embarrassed for having shown fear.

Slowly, he leaned forward until their faces were only inches apart.

In a growling whisper, he said, "You are traveling down a dangerous road, Lori. Very, *very* dangerous.

If I'm the one to show you that, so be it. *Oh*, and get some pants without holes in them."

With that, he turned and walked away, his pristinely white tennis shoes squeaking as he disappeared into the shadows. Lori watched him go and felt the humming adrenaline fade from her body. She almost couldn't believe she'd talked to a teacher like that, especially one as intimidating as Coach Teller, but she was proud. She'd stood up for herself and her band.

"Is he gone?" a voice whispered.

Lori looked down to find Meadow sticking her head out of the small trapdoor just a few feet away. With the door open, it definitely smelled like pot smoke. Teller had been right about that, at least.

"We heard the whole thing. Thanks for running interference," Meadow said.

Then Memphis popped up behind her, barely able to wedge himself through the tight space with her in it.

"Yeah, thanks, Lori. That was badass," he said with a big, silly grin. "He's a knob. Your jeans are sweet."

Lori nodded in agreement. She thought her torn-up jeans complemented her Ugly Kid Joe t-shirt and flannel overshirt just fine.

"*Whoa*, guys!"

All three of them turned to Seth, walking back onstage with his fuzz pedal in hand. He scrunched up his nose.

"It reeks of weed in here!" he half-whispered, and all three of them broke out in laughter.

"Get outta the hole you two, we've got to play like, *now*," Lori said.

The rhythm section climbed out, and they scrambled to take their places.

Lori pulled a tape recorder from her pocket and placed it a few feet away from her amp. She carried the recorder with her everywhere, just in case inspiration struck and she wanted to hum a tune or record a new riff. She recorded their live shows, too. The sound quality wasn't great, but it was good enough that she could listen back and see where they could tighten up their stage sound.

She'd barely pressed the record button before the curtain rose and the stage lights were blinding them, and kids were yelling. Some cheers, some joking requests for "Free Bird." The nerves rose and fell in her stomach, and she wished she'd been able to complete her backstage meditation.

She pushed through the fear and launched into their first song, "Breathe," with staccato strums on a power chord. She sang close to the mic, her voice low and husky. Memphis' drum beats came slow and creeping. Meadow's bass created a sludgy drone. Seth stood stock still, cool and waiting. When they hit the chorus, all of them exploded into a pounding, heavy rhythm that was still melodic and hooky. That was when Seth came in, adding buzzsaw wails that lifted the chorus, adding a new dynamic and texture—a new power.

As Lori played the song she'd sung dozens of times before, she looked out at the audience before them. Kids danced, raising their fists and bobbing their heads.

She had loved this music her whole life. Bands like Hüsker Dü, and the Replacements, and Patti Smith, and Fugazi made her feel less alone. Picking up a guitar and playing their songs herself made her feel like she could do something with her life. But her classmates? A year before, the same kids dancing to her original songs had called Lori a spazz, and a nerd, and worse. Then Nirvana had blown up MTV like an atomic bomb, and suddenly, grunge—alternative rock or whatever you wanted to call it—was cool.

There was Callie Green, who had been Lori's friend in fifth grade until she came over to play and saw that Lori lived in a trailer. There was Ryan Dunmore, who had made jokes about Lori's body to the whole bus on an eighth-grade trip to Washington, D.C. Then there was Ellen Cliff. She'd tricked Lori into using Nair on her scalp, telling her it was fancy French shampoo in ninth grade. All of them now danced to her music and called out her name like they were friends.

As far as Lori was concerned, her only *true* friends were the ones on stage with her, the ones who believed in her dream and wanted to share it and the ones who backed her up. She would do anything for them.

"Breathe" ended in a wall of fuzzy feedback. Lori wiped sweat off her brow and checked in with the band. Meadow gave her a big grin. The bass player had held it down, bouncing and jumping around behind her. Meadow had more energy than all of them combined, and she brought it to the stage every time they played. Memphis gave an apologetic look.

He'd dragged and fallen behind a bit. A habit of his that tended to happen when he'd smoked. Lori knew he was beating himself up about it already. She gave him a thumbs up and mouthed, "It's okay." He nodded, but she could tell he didn't believe her. Finally, she gave Seth a quick look. He nodded too, cool and confident, but not cocky. He'd killed it, like always, but didn't show off.

During the quiet lull in the music, a single voice rose above the murmurs and occasional hollers. It was a high-pitched, excited voice crying out, "Seth! Seth!"

Lori looked to find a group of moms standing by the table with the punch and snacks. She recognized them immediately as the "PTA Moms," a group of ladies infamous throughout the school for their constant pledge drives, club patronages, and other school-sponsored activities like *Students Against Litter* and *No-Cursing Tuesdays*. For the latter, every student caught cursing on Tuesdays had to put a dollar in a swear jar located in the school's main office. This particular initiative had already raised over a thousand dollars.

Lori found them to be annoying and uptight, but she couldn't be too mad at them. They were the ones who had asked Crying Lilacs to play the Spring Fling that they'd organized for the students. The band had been surprised and a bit reticent, but said yes when they realized there was a decent payment attached to their performance.

That night, all the PTA Moms were perfectly made up with expensive hairdos and nice, but conservative, outfits. None were done up as well as Julie

Haggerty, Seth's mom. If anyone didn't know that she was Seth's mom, she made it immediately clear by screaming, "That's my son! *Woo-hoo!* Crying Lilacs *rocks*!" in a pronounced Southern accent.

Across the stage, Seth shot Lori an embarrassed, pleading look, as if to say, "Please start the next song now, I can't handle this." Lori understood, but couldn't feel too bad for him. Not that she wanted her own mother to cause a scene like that, but it would have been nice for her to show up at all, to anything that Lori had ever done with her band.

She took pity on Seth and leaned into the microphone.

"This next one is called 'Fall Into Me.' It's a slow one, so you get close. But leave room for Jesus."

Some of the kids laughed as she played the slow, shimmering open chords of the song's beginning. Meadow and Memphis locked into an easy groove behind her. Seth's playing, as always, complemented hers perfectly, delicately dancing over her chords, accentuating her yearning lyrics.

The lights in the gymnasium had dimmed, and she watched as her fellow students held each other and moved to the rhythm. She wondered if they were falling in love to the soundtrack of her band's songs. She wondered if they would remember this moment forever. She wondered if she would, and hoped it would be replaced by something bigger, better. Something far away from this school and the parents and the teachers, and her suffocating little town.

Suddenly, Lori got the feeling that she was being watched. Not in the way that someone watches a band perform, but *stared at*. She scanned the big room . . .

There. In the back.

Blake Cutler stood along the far wall of the gym, wearing his letterman jacket over a polo shirt. His football buddies stood next to him, exuding an arrogance particular to all jocks that Lori had come to despise. Blake was many things: a star quarterback, one of the top five cutest guys at Roosevelt High, and Lori's angry, jealous ex who blamed her for the end of their relationship.

Blake Cutler was glaring at her, unblinking, with the most fiery anger she'd ever seen.

He looked like he wanted to kill her.

Chapter 3

Lori's heart fluttered in her chest. The show had gone perfectly—well, almost. Blake's death stare was still unsettling, but she did her best to push it from her mind and to focus on the crowd's cheers as she loaded the amps into the van.

It was the beginning of spring, and the cool night air felt good as it dried the sweat of the show on her skin. Beside her, Memphis loaded his disassembled drum kit. He slid in the last of the cymbals and took a breather, leaning against the van. He dug in his pocket for a moment and came up with a pack of Pall Mall Red cigarettes. He tapped one out for himself and held out the pack to Lori.

"Smoke?"

Lori nodded gratefully and took one.

"You only live once," she said as she placed it between her lips.

Memphis pulled a lighter from his pocket, a silver Zippo with the Kiss logo etched into the side. They all laughed at the corny makeup and theatrics, but secretly enjoyed the arena rock anthems. The flame came to life and illuminated his face in the night. It was a strange, eerie visual that made Lori feel uneasy in a way that she couldn't explain.

"Hey, I wanted to say . . . *um* . . ." Memphis kicked at the cracked black asphalt with the dirty toe of his Chuck Taylor. "I'm sorry I fell behind again tonight. I'm gonna get some extra rehearsing done this week, I promise. I'll, like, play to the timer thing."

A metronome, Lori thought, but didn't correct him. She took his lighter and lit her own smoke. She put her hand on Memphis' shoulder and looked him in the eyes. In them, she saw so much insecurity, a deep need to be welcomed and loved. He'd been cast aside by other people in his life, she knew. That's why the band was there. They'd all been failed by people in their lives who were supposed to be there for them. Well, all of them except for Seth. He had it all together.

"It's okay man, you were great. You sounded like thunder out there tonight."

Memphis brushed his hair from his face and said, "I'll do better, Lori. This is really important to me."

"Memphis, look at me, dude. As long as you want to be in this band, you'll be in this band. We're not going anywhere without you."

Memphis smiled. He didn't speak. He didn't have to, she knew what he was thinking.

Suddenly, something landed on her back, and she staggered forward, barely keeping her balance on the asphalt. Meadow wrapped her arms around Lori's neck, playfully bit into her ear, and let out a growl. Laughing, Lori shook her friend off and hugged her.

"You were freaking awesome tonight!" Meadow gushed.

"You were!" Lori replied happily and shook Meadow off her.

"They were eating out of the palm of our hands like little dogs! We owned that room!" Meadow paced back and forth, a ball of excited energy. "Those kids used to bully us, and now they love us. If we can win them over, we can play any club, any bar, any *arena* in this stupid country!" She spun around and fixed her ecstatic gaze on Lori. "We should go party! Joe Flanders is throwing a banger. They'll treat us like gods after that show."

"Is JoEllen gonna be there?" Memphis asked around his cigarette. "She's so pretty, dude."

"*Everybody's* gonna be there. You're coming with me. Lori, you in?"

"I dunno, I'm feeling pretty productive. Like, excited, you know? I think I wanna go home and do a little writing." Lori patted the tape recorder in her pocket. She was committed to holding firm. Meadow had a way of getting people to bend to her enthusiasm.

"Besides," Lori added as extra ammo in her defense, "Somebody's gotta take the equipment back to the space. We can't leave it in the van overnight, we'll get ripped off."

"I'll help you," Seth called. He was walking across the parking lot, his guitar case in one hand, coils of cable in the other. The real baggage, though, came in the form of his mother, who trailed behind him, beaming with pride.

Lori rolled her eyes and gave Memphis a look. Time to put out the smokes. In perfect unison, they dropped them to the ground, toed them out beneath their sneakers, and shared a secret little grin.

Seth stepped between them to slide his guitar into the tightly packed puzzle of equipment stashed in the back of the van. "Thanks guys," he said quietly.

"You got it." Memphis slapped him on the back.

"You kids were so good tonight!" Seth's mom gushed breathlessly in her lilting accent. "I mean it. Lori, such a beautiful voice! Your lyrics are so, *um*, what's the word . . . Edgy? Yes, that's it. Very edgy. I didn't realize when I booked y'all." She laughed heartily, "I might have to smooth some ruffled feathers, but boy howdy, I don't regret it."

"Thanks, Mom, for coming and all, but we gotta go."

Not everyone noticed the subtle change in Seth when his mother came around, but Lori did. He always got a little tense, a little nervous. Who could blame him? The woman was an Apache helicopter of adult supervision. She was super positive, but it was all so overwhelming that it became weirdly oppressive.

"Yeah, we're all going to a party," Meadow chimed in.

Subtle, Lori thought.

"*Oh*, yes. Well, okay," Julie seemed suddenly befuddled. A bit lost. "I'll go and let you kids have fun. Be home by ten, Seth. And please, sweetie, no drinking. That goes for all you kids. Nothing good happens after midnight, you know?"

Julie held up both hands and waved, then turned on her high-heeled pumps and walked away, deeper into the school's parking lot, murmuring to herself about where she may have parked.

As soon as she was gone, Seth seemed to relax a bit. "Sorry, guys. She's just *really* supportive."

"Yeah, that was a lot," Meadow said. "*Aaaanyway*, who's coming to this party?!"

Before anyone could answer, the four of them were hit with blinding high beams. They looked in the direction of the light's source, but couldn't make out the car through the glaring light. An engine revved, and the car raced toward them.

"*Oh* my god," Lori said, a gasp caught in her throat. "They're not going to stop!"

Lori closed her eyes and braced for impact. *Is this how I go? In the freaking parking lot of Roosevelt High?*

Screeeeech!

At the very last moment, the driver slammed on the brakes.

The car fishtailed, then went into a controlled skid. Tires squealing and smoking on the pavement, the car whipped around until the driver's side was aligned with the back of the van and came to a sudden, hard stop.

As the glare faded and smoke cleared from Lori's vision, she was able to identify the car. A brand new Dodge Viper convertible, and Blake Cutler laughed behind the wheel. It sounded cruel, like a blade on a grinding wheel.

"You like it, Lori? I just got it!"

"How much did your dad fork over for it?" Lori asked with a smirk.

Blake's expression darkened.

"You know, I don't understand why you won't just

talk to me. You dump me with a note in my locker and then you just go silent? That's cowardly behavior, Lori. You're better than that."

Memphis and Seth both stepped forward in a protective gesture. Lori appreciated the thought, but it made her a little embarrassed. She hated feeling dependent on the protection of others.

"I have nothing to say to you."

Even through the shadows, Lori could see Blake's hands flex as he tightened his grip around the steering wheel, his knuckles whitened. He nearly shook with a rage that simmered just below the surface.

"You're my girl, Lori. How about you let me decide when you have nothing to say?"

"That doesn't make any sense," Meadow interjected.

"Shut up, freak!" Blake scowled at Meadow. Then, like a ventriloquist doll suddenly changing his expression, his lips flipped into a wide, cheesy grin. He turned to Lori. "Come on, babe, just get in the car. We'll go for a ride. I'll let you work my stick."

Lori walked toward the car. She leaned down to the window and looked him dead in the eyes. She could smell the sour reek of cheap beer and cheaper whiskey wafting from him and remembered one of the reasons why she'd called it off with him.

Through gritted teeth, she said, "You wanna talk? The Lori you dated is gone. I'm a new person now. You'd be riding with a stranger." She turned to go, then stopped and looked back. "I . . . and Blake, if you ever talk to Meadow like that again, you'll be driving home with a broken stick. Got it? Get outta here."

Blake's face twisted into a mask of humiliation and rage. For a moment, it looked like he was about to get out of the car, but he remained in the vehicle.

He stabbed his index finger at Lori. "We're not done. We're not over. You don't get over me. I won't let you."

He hit the gas, and the Viper peeled away, leaving skid marks on the pavement.

"Sorry, I don't mean to be rude, but what did you see in that guy?" Seth asked.

Lori didn't want to tell him the truth: It had felt good to be seen with him. That, before she'd found her own voice, her own style, she had relied on Blake and his social status to make her feel like more than just another no-future girl from the trailer park. She'd barely been able to admit that to herself, much less anyone else. Now that she had her voice, she felt she'd earned the right to keep it to herself.

"I don't know," she said simply.

"Well, whatever good quality he had, I think it's gone now," Meadow said. "He's really dangerous, Lori."

Lori knew she was right.

Chapter 4

Lori sat in the passenger seat of Seth's van as they drove through the night, gliding beneath the shadows cast by the sweetgum trees lining the old state highway. She rolled the window down and let the mild spring air whip through her long hair.

Memphis had left his pack of cigarettes with her when he and Meadow went to Joe Flander's party, and she tapped one out between her fingers. She slipped the smoke between her lips and then froze, giving Seth a questioning look.

He hesitated, then grinned and said, "It's fine."

"Thanks. It's been a long night."

Blake's sneering face filled her mind. For a second, she could smell the noxious odor of rubber on asphalt as the Viper peeled away, tires screeching. She shook away the vision, lit up the cigarette, and let the sweet night's air sweep the smoke away with all the bad thoughts.

"Lori, there's something I need to confess to you," Seth said quietly. His face was grave in the pale moonlight, slashing through the windshield. "Something I should have told you a long time ago, but I . . . I just couldn't."

Filled with dread, Lori answered, "What . . . what is it, Seth?"

"I . . . I . . . I have no idea why our drummer goes by Memphis." He couldn't hold his act together anymore, and his stony expression cracked into a broad grin. "Seriously, that name is crazy!"

Relieved, Lori giggled and punched him in the arm. "You jerk, you really had me worried for a sec!"

"I'm sorry," he said, still laughing. "For real though, is that his legal name?"

"It is, actually. And it's a big part of who he is. His story, you know? It's really personal for him. Not my story to tell."

"I'm sorry, I didn't know. I thought it was just a funny nickname."

Lori said, "It's okay. You really had me, dude," and laughed.

They rode in easy silence for a few more miles until Seth pulled off the two-lane country blacktop and onto a narrow dirt road that cut between two cotton fields and led into a thicket of trees beyond. Seth navigated the van down the bumpy little road and through the tree line until they reached a ramshackle barn.

The band's rehearsal space.

The van's headlights illuminated it in the night until Seth stopped and cut the engine, casting the world around them into darkness. They got out of the van. While Seth began unloading everything, Lori unlocked the double padlocks and stepped inside the barn.

She breathed deeply, taking in the earthy odor of the place, the dust and wood. It was old and didn't look like much. Its clapboard exterior had once been painted a bright red, but it was now faded and weather-beaten. The interior was a bit rundown, too, but it had good bones and solid doors to keep their gear safe.

She was grateful to Tucker Woodlawn, the farmer who owned the land near the trailer park she lived at. She'd known him for years, ever since she was a little girl. One day, she bumped into him on the road, and the kindly old man had let her borrow the barn for as long as she and the band needed it.

Now the walls were covered in band posters and egg crates Memphis had stapled up. He'd claimed the crates would help with the acoustics. None of them had ever noticed the difference, but they left them up.

The barn was Lori's safe space. She never felt more protected or creative than when she was there.

Seth brushed gently past her, a guitar case hanging in each hand. He set them carefully down on the cracked concrete floor.

"*Oh*, do you need help? Sorry, I got a little lost in thought."

"It's fine," he said. "I pulled everything out of the van if you wanna grab the amps and I can get the—"

"Actually, I wanna hang here for a bit. I like the peace and quiet. I'll carry everything in and walk home." She saw a quick flash of worry pass over his face. *He doesn't want me to walk home alone in the dark*, she thought. "I'll be okay," she added.

"Don't forget to lock up."

"Never."

"Good show," he said. "You were awesome up there."

"You too," she said, and meant it.

He patted her on the shoulder and headed out the door. She listened as his footsteps receded into the shadows. He fired up the van's engine and pulled away into the night.

She stepped outside where the rest of the equipment sat. The open country surrounded her. The inky black sky. Everything was so big, and she was so small.

Lori felt like the whole world was going to close in and swallow her whole.

When Lori returned home, the trailer was dark, and the front door was ajar. She always reminded her mother, Amber, to lock it, but sometimes the booze got the better of her, and she didn't pay attention to her surroundings. Still, it was unusual for the door to actually be open.

Could someone have broken in?

Lori put her ear to the crack and listened. For a long moment, there was only an eerie silence as she tuned her hearing. Then she picked up on some subtle sounds: her mother's irregular snores and the low hum of the television.

She shook her head as she stepped inside and pulled the door tight behind her, flicking the dead bolt hard.

Maybe it was the strange feeling she'd gotten standing out in front of the barn, or the walk home through the shadowy woods, but a slow, haunting melody had begun playing in Lori's head on the way home, and she wanted to record it before she forgot it. She'd left the Jaguar in the barn as her only amp was there as well, but that was okay. She could hum the tune straight into the tape recorder.

The TV glowed blue in the living room, flickering with an infomercial about how to make enough money to buy a mansion with a pool and a jet with a fleet of beautiful flight attendants.

Amber drooled on the sofa. Light brown hair, turning prematurely gray, lay around her head in a tousled halo. She was wearing nothing but a pair of faded underwear and a baggy t-shirt with Ziggy screenprinted on it.

A bottle of wine lay empty on the carpet next to her.

Lori took a crumpled afghan off the stained recliner and draped it around her mother. She turned off the TV. She kissed her fingertip and pressed it gently against the sleeping woman's forehead, then hurried quietly from the room before Amber stirred awake from her stupor and began to grill her about where she'd been.

Lori slipped into her cramped room in the back of the trailer. There was barely enough space for her twin-size bed, a small dresser, and her stacks of music magazines. All over the room were piles of *Rolling Stone* and *Ray Gun*, *Melody Maker* and *Maximum Rocknroll*, some of them dating back years. Some she had bought herself with money scraped together from odd jobs and Crying Lilacs gigs, but many had been given to her by her dad. Ever since she was a little girl, she'd loved going through them. She read every article in detail, practiced all the poses of her favorite stars in the mirror, and dreamed of the day she would be in them herself.

The trailer had always been their family home, but when her father, Cameron, was alive, he'd had plans to move them to a bigger place. He had dreamed of leaving the Pep Boys, where he worked as a mechanic, and opening up his own shop. He would drive Lori around the suburbs and point out modest ranch houses, telling her his plans to buy one for the family. A *proper home* was what he'd called them.

That was before the cancer took him away. Before her mother became so lost in grief that she fell into the bottle and never came back.

Everything was different now. If Lori wanted her father's dream to come true, she'd have to do it herself.

She sat down on her bed, and her mattress sagged under her. She pulled the tape recorder from her pocket and held it to her lips.

She pressed record and began to sing the haunting melody she carried home with her.

Chapter 5

Lori opened her eyes. She stood alone in a field. All around her were dead and dying cotton plants. The dessicated white bolls barely clung to their spindly branches. She had no idea how she had gotten there. The soil beneath her feet was soft and moist. The air was cool, and she shivered against it. She wrapped her arms around herself and realized that she wasn't wearing a shirt. She looked down and saw nothing but her own pale skin.

What was she doing naked in a field?

Panic gripped her. Her heart pounded like a double bass drum. Her breath came in shallow, ragged gasps.

Her eyes darted across the landscape around her. There were no trees. No houses. No roads or cars. She was surrounded by farming fields full of withered, lifeless crops that were once corn, tobacco, and even more cotton. Death surrounded her.

Suddenly, a brightness appeared on the horizon. A small cluster of twinkling lights. They illuminated a home. Not a mansion, nothing fancy. A small, suburban house. Still, it was a world away from her own.

A feeling of safety emanated from those lights.

She knew, somehow, that if she could get there, she would be okay.

The moment she took her first step forward, a hand erupted from the earth in front of her. Pale white, decaying flesh covered the bony appendage, all the way down to the shoulder. It gripped her around her ankle.

A scream froze in her throat. The arm squeezed her tightly, impossibly tight, despite being practically skeletal.

She tried to kick free with her bare feet, but then a second arm tore from the dirt and grabbed her other leg. Then she did scream—an anguished cry more powerful than any sound she'd ever made behind the microphone. With animalistic desperation, she kicked against the hands, but they would not let go.

She reached down and grabbed the fingers wrapped around her right leg, cold and bony. She pulled at them with all her strength until, one by one, they snapped bloodlessly off. Disgusted, she flung them into the field.

After desperately—violently—pulling off more fingers from each hand, she finally got free.

As she broke into a run, more zombified arms popped up through the field. Hundreds of them appeared in unison, growing from the soil like springtime in hell, and grasped violently at the air. Their flesh was rotten with pustulating abscesses. Their filthy fingernails were torn back, revealing bleeding, scabrous nail beds.

Lori picked up her knees and ran through the field, dodging the flailing, grasping hands.

It felt like she was gaining ground, but no matter

how far she ran, she never seemed to make it any closer to the warm lights of the distant house.

Then another hand managed to grip her ankle. Lori went down, landing amongst the horrible hands, which grabbed her by the arms and legs, pinning her to the earth.

"Help! Help me, please!" she howled into the night.

She felt the soft earth beneath her begin to give and realized that the hands of these buried ghouls weren't just trying to pin her to the dirt. They were pulling her beneath it.

As she sank into the soil, she felt bugs and worms crawl against her flesh. She fought to keep her head above ground as her body was pulled under. She gasped for air. She screamed and screamed. But she knew it was no use.

She would never get to the bright, warm, loving lights. She knew it even before the dirt filled her screaming mouth.

Lori awoke to laughter. She whipped her head up and looked around at a classroom full of kids, all pointing at her. She blinked in the harsh yellow lights. She'd fallen asleep in class. *Again*. And had a nightmare. She's probably been talking or screaming in her sleep. *Great*.

At the front of the room, Mr. Tomlinson stood before a large medical diagram of a uterus and regarded her with an irritated air, as if this were expected from someone like Lori. Someone from the trailer park.

She couldn't decide which was worse, being

buried alive by zombies or being in sex ed with Mr. Tomlinson.

He narrowed his piggish eyes behind thick-rimmed glasses. "Catching up on your beauty sleep, Miss Levi?"

Lori glanced up at him, still bleary-eyed and disoriented. "*Huh?*"

"*Huh?*" he repeated in a mocking tone. He ran his fingers through his sandy mustache and licked his chapped lips. "How would you like to come to the front of class and teach your friends about, *uh . . .*" he looked at the diagram behind him, "Fallopian tubes?"

"*Ew*, don't use that word. Creep."

Meadow giggled from the seat behind her. Lori turned around to her friend. "Shut up," she hissed.

Mr. Tomlinson's pockmarked face twisted up in anger, and he stepped toward her. He froze when the bell sounded, causing a flurry of insanity as all the kids immediately forgot the current drama in their rush to get out of the glass.

"Saved by the bell, Miss Levi," Mr. Tomlinson said. He jerked his head toward the door. "Get out."

Grateful for the interruption, Lori grabbed her backpack and hurried out into the hall with Meadow. They moved into the chaotic throngs of students going this way and that, like ants rushing around to please the queen.

Meadow sidled up next to Lori and elbowed her in the arm. "You really gave it to Tomlinson in there.

"I regret nothing," Lori said. "He *is* a creep. I don't know why he's teaching sex ed to begin with. Like he knows anything about what goes on in a woman's body. He's probably a virgin."

Meadow and Lori laughed together.

Meadow asked, "What kept you up last night? Dreaming of Seth?"

"*Oh*, please. I was working on a new song, actually."

"I don't know how you do it. Write all these songs, I mean. Whenever I sit down to try and get what's in my head out, I like just . . . freeze up. Like it won't translate or something. Good thing I'm just the bass player. Less stress."

It was then they both noticed that the fervor of the hallway had died down. They were the only students left. Immediately, they realized their predicament.

In unison, they turned to each other and said, "We're late."

Lori thought it over for a minute and said, "Wanna skip? We can drive around, and I can play you the song on my recorder. It's rough, but . . ."

"I've got some Super Skunk that'll smooth all of it out," Meadow joked.

Lori snickered, threw her arm around Meadow's shoulders, and together they began to walk toward the exit leading to the parking lot. A familiar voice made them stop in their tracks.

"Stop what you're doing *now*!" the tinny voice came in over the loudspeaker. It was, unmistakably, the voice of Seth's mother, the eternally chipper Julie Haggerty.

"*Oh* god," Meadow whispered. "She knows we were talking about him. She's been listening."

43

Lori giggled and put a finger to her lips, shushing her friend.

"That's right," Julie continued over the loudspeaker. "Stop what you're doing because I have news for you! Roosevelt High has been chosen to participate in a nationwide Battle of the Bands competition, and we at the PTA are delighted to invite all of you to take the stage at the event we're hosting in just two weeks! The winners will represent our beloved little town at a nationwide competition that will air live on television. They may also win a record contract. So mark your calendars and start rehearsing!"

With a staticky *click*, Julie's voice went quiet. Lori and Meadow looked at each other in disbelief. *A live concert on television? A record deal?* Lori grabbed Meadow and pulled her into a big hug.

"This is it," Lori whispered in her friend's ear. "This is everything."

Chapter 6

That day, the springtime weather had officially taken hold. Pleasant and mild. Lori had happily walked the several miles from Roosevelt High to the rehearsal space.

Sweat was pouring off her as she walked up the dirt road to the barn. She wiped her brow and took a quick sniff of her pits. *Barf*, she thought to herself.

Whatever. She had bigger fish to fry. Nobody would care what she smelled like or whether her hair was in perfect place once she got famous. Kurt Cobain looked like he reeked, and nobody told Kathleen Hanna or Donita Sparks to fix their hair. And if they did, they probably got punched in the mouth.

Lori was grinning at that idea. *Soon enough, that will be me*, she decided. Then she corrected herself. *It will be all of us*. She knew she had a tendency to center herself in all of her fantasies. It was a normal thing to do, but she needed to keep her band members in her heart as well.

All they had to do was win the Battle of the Bands, and everyone in Crying Lilacs would be living the rockstar life. Much more importantly, they would be making art that people really connected with. Art that would reach more than a handful around Red Elm, North Carolina.

That is far more important, she thought. *I can help people like me feel a little less alone.*

If they kept their heads up and practiced, nothing could stop them from winning the Battle. There was barely even any competition standing in their way.

Lori was grinning to herself when she got to the door of the barn, and then she stopped dead in her tracks. Somebody had cut both of their security padlocks. They swung uselessly in their latches. The old wooden door hung open.

"*Oh no! Oh no, no, no!*" she whispered under her breath.

She had a sudden flash of the night before when she had stood at the open door of the trailer.

Lori pulled her keys out of her pocket and clenched them in her fist. The trailer key jutted out like a wicked talon. She leaned in, pressing her face into the crack between the door and the wall. The sun-baked wood was hot and rough against her cheeks. She peered into the murky darkness of the barn.

No movement.

Fighting the terror down, she raised her voice and called out, "Listen, jerk! If you wanna steal our equipment, you're outta luck. I will kill you for that guitar. So just move on, man."

No reply came. Only eerie quiet.

Lori pulled the door open and took a tentative step inside, fists raised. It took a moment for her eyes to adjust to the darkness, but when they did, and she saw what had been done, she gasped in horror.

Their equipment had been destroyed. All of it.

Amps were kicked in. Drums were crushed, cymbals dented beyond recognition. Seth's guitar and Meadow's bass were broken at their necks. Worst of all was the Jaguar. Lori's baby had been bashed to death on the concrete floor. The neck was snapped, the body was cracked. The attacker had even managed to rip the pickups out. They hung by their wires like viscera ripped from a body, clinging only by dying connective tissue and veins.

Lori didn't realize she was crying until the hot tears fell on her cheeks.

Something clattered in the darkness. It sounded like something metallic clanking upon the concrete.

Lori looked in the direction of the noise. At first, she didn't see it, lurking in the shadows. Then she locked eyes with it.

A figure, standing in the dark, watching her from behind a featureless black mask.

Chapter 7

The figure stood about ten feet away from her in the shadows of the barn, near a wall where old farming implements hung. They were clad in a black, hooded robe. Beneath the robe was black tactical-style clothing: boots, cargo pants, and a turtleneck. The mask was a featureless ebony void, save for two small eye holes, just big enough for Lori to make out the person's sinister gaze.

As she looked into the terrifying mask, she tried to find a detail that she could remember, something to hold onto to identify the creep later. The eyes were blue? Green? Gray? She couldn't tell in the dim light.

The only thing she knew for sure was that whoever was behind the mask was very, *very* dangerous.

Lori broke eye contact with the creep just long enough to grab Meadow's broken bass neck from the floor and brandish it like a club. If she was going down, she would go down swinging.

She considered screaming for help, but the barn was in the middle of nowhere. Besides, nobody ever came to help anyway. What good would it do?

There was a long, tense moment where both of

them silently studied each other. *Is the creep armed? Will they attack me? Who is it behind that mask?*

The creep said nothing. They didn't move.

She could hear them breathing heavily behind the mask.

From the time she'd entered the barn till now, it had only been a minute at most, but it felt like an eternity.

"I'll kick your ass, dude," Lori said, trying her best to sound menacing.

A choked, wet laugh emanated from behind the mask. Then, more heavy breathing.

Suddenly, the creep reached to the wall near them and pulled down a rusty old lawnmower blade from a hook. They flung it at Lori. It whistled through the air toward her, but she ducked and leapt out of the way of the blade's arc.

The creep ran to the door, yanked it open, and took off out of the barn.

Lori sprinted after them. She stopped in the doorway and looked out into the night. The figure was gone.

Still clutching the bass neck in her hand, Lori staggered back into the barn. She pulled the door closed, grabbed an old lawn chair, and wedged it up under a board on the back of the door to hold it closed. It wasn't much, but it might slow down her attacker if they came back.

She kicked at the lawnmower blade that now lay on the cracked cement floor. The thing was practically an antique. So blunt that it wouldn't have done much to her if it had connected with her. Whoever it was hadn't come prepared to do her harm, but they were prepared to try if cornered.

Lori tried her best to remain composed as she took in the mess of broken instruments strewn around her, but she couldn't shake the thought.

"Jesus, Lori, are you okay? I mean, did you go to the hospital?" Seth asked her, eyes wide with concern and fear. He was sitting on top of one of the broken amps in the barn, and his legs hung in the air. It made him look like a little boy. Lori found it endearing.

She looked up from the Jaguar. Some of the wires attaching the guitar's humbucker had come loose, and she was putting them back together with a soldering gun.

"No, they didn't actually hurt me."

"No, but like, yeah, like a psychiatrist or something," Memphis said. He was pacing back and forth around the area where his bashed drum kit had been scattered, hopelessly examining each piece to see what was salvageable and coming up empty. "Being abused can hurt your brain more than your body sometimes. Ms. Wilkins told me that," he added.

Meadow stood in the corner, arms wrapped around herself in a hug. "I hate to admit this, but I'm scared, you guys. Who would want to do this?"

Lori spoke through gritted teeth. "Anyone. Someone from a rival band . . . It sounds corny, but it could be somebody who just hates rock n' roll . . . Coach Teller, that guy hates us and everything we stand for."

"Blake," Memphis offered.

Oh, god, Lori thought. *Blake*. This is exactly the kind of mean-spirited thing he would do as he escalated in his anger over her dumping him. But would he really have thrown a lawnmower blade at her?

Meadow continued, "Now I really hate to say this, but . . . should we call the cops?"

"The cops?" Lori scoffed.

The only thing she'd seen the cops around their town do was show up to evict her neighbors in the trailer park and pull people over to raise their traffic fine quotas and try to catch kids with a little beer or weed so they could rough them up and, of course, collect even more fines.

"Hey now, the cops could really help. I know it's not cool or whatever, but this is what they're here for," Seth said. His voice was patient and kind. Trying not to push.

"Maybe the cops help people in your neighborhood, but not kids like us," Memphis said, then quickly added, "No offense."

"Fair enough. But then what do we do here?" Seth asked Lori. "This feels dangerous . . ."

Lori looked up at Seth. Then at Meadow and Memphis. She realized that they were all looking at her, waiting for guidance. For a brief moment, she resented it. She wished they would just dive in on their own and do what she was doing, pick up the pieces, and keep going. But, she knew, she was the leader. She needed to step up. Besides, they were her family—her *real* family—and they needed her help, just like she needed them.

She forced herself to put her anger aside. She had to be steady.

"What do we do?" Lori said it rhetorically. "We rebuild. Some of this is salvageable . . . Maybe. What isn't we'll beg, borrow, or steal to replace. This jerk, whoever they are, thought this would be enough to take us down? No way. We're going to keep going. We're going to win the Battle of the Bands, we're going to win the national competition, and we're going to get that record deal."

"Hell yeah!" Memphis shouted.

Meadow was beaming. Lori could see the fear was melting away from her friend. "You're right. We're gonna do this," Meadow said.

Seth didn't say anything. He silently locked eyes with Lori, and she could feel the encouragement radiating off him. It felt like he was really proud of her, and that meant the world to her.

She knew with this crew together and committed, they really could win. She wanted to celebrate. To get out of the hard work for just a bit and show them all how much she loved them.

"But first, let's have some fun," Lori said.

"Crying Lilacs is never gonna die!" Lori hollered as she leapt off the cliff.

Meadow and Memphis stood behind her in the late afternoon sun, cheering her on as she swung out over the water on the old rope that had been hanging there from before she was even born. As she let go, she let out a *whoop* and cannonballed into the water just a few feet from where Seth was treading.

The cold liquid struck her and made her tense up in shock. It took her body a moment to adjust. When it did, she kicked her powerful legs and reached for the surface of the water. As she came up from beneath, she blinked water from her eyes and found that she was floating right in front of Seth. He was treading water comfortably in the spot they called the Elephant Hole. It was a small body of water nestled in a forest of poplar trees, fed by a healthy diet of rain and runoff from a nearby creek. Generations of kids had gone swimming there and had their first kiss, their first beer, and more than that.

Seth hadn't taken the rope. Instead, he'd walked into the water from the security of the shore beneath the little cliff overlooking the water.

"Safety first, *huh?*" she asked him.

Typical, serious Seth. "I heard this story that years back, this kid, around our age, he jumped in here like you just did. But he dove in, went super deep, cracked his head open on a big rock down there."

"I think I heard this . . ."

The story of the kid who'd hurt himself diving into the Elephant Hole had been around for years. An urban legend. A rural legend in Red Elm. She never knew his name or age, but it was always a teenage boy. The damage was always a little different, too. In some tellings, he was a quadriplegic. In others, he was brain-damaged or dead.

"I think adults made that up to scare kids," Lori said.

"No, it's true," Seth said firmly. "He hit so hard it, like, rewired his brain, so that his identity is just gone. Mind wipe. He can't even talk. He sits in a chair all day and stares out the window of a state hospital. I don't want to be a vegetable."

"Good. I'm more of a meat and potatoes girl myself."

Seth rolled his eyes in an exaggerated way. "Too soon! Poor taste!"

She knew he was joking, but she did feel a little bad about it. If the story were true, if the boy really had gotten stuck in some hospital here, she couldn't think of anything worse. Trapped in this town with no ability to express yourself? She shivered.

"Are you cold?" Seth asked. "Your body will adjust to the water in a sec."

"No, no, I'm fine, just thinking . . . Don't worry about it."

She tried to get her mind off the thought and looked up at the cliff where Meadow and Memphis were playfully fighting over who got to go next on the rope.

She treaded water beside Seth and realized suddenly that they were both in their underwear. She'd gone to the Elephant Hole so many times with Meadow and Memphis that she didn't even think about it. The three of them were like siblings. Seth was . . . different.

She started to feel a little self-conscious and let herself sink a bit deeper so that even her shoulders were covered beneath the water.

"Okay, I'm just gonna say it," Seth said. "It's a *little* awkward that we're all in our underwear in front of each other."

Oh my god, it's like he's reading my mind, Lori thought. But she didn't say that. Instead, she shrugged and said, "It's whatever. We're a family, no big deal."

"I guess."

"... all right, it is a little weird," she admitted.

Seth let out a big laugh. He pulled his arm way back and brought it crashing down, splashing her with a wave.

"*Agh!* Seth!" She splashed him back.

She was trying to be playful; she wanted to just have fun, but she couldn't stop thinking about the legend Seth had brought up. The image of a young kid sentenced to live a life like that . . . It scared her worse than any knife-wielding maniac.

"Seth . . . that story about the boy . . . Do you really believe it's true?"

His face became sullen. "I don't believe it, I know it," he said. "It's true."

He opened his mouth to say more, but then they heard Meadow holler out from above. She let go of the rope and, still hooting, came crashing down on Lori, taking her underwater with her.

Chapter 8

Lori didn't understand why Seth hadn't told her the truth. Not that he'd lied. Not exactly. He'd just omitted some things.

The Jaguar was almost back up to playing speed; she was just waiting for the glue to set around the guitar's neck. It was at home now, in her bedroom, with a plastic clamp holding it together. But her amp was hopeless, totally dead, and Seth hadn't said anything about having a spare one.

The PTA mothers had money. Everyone knew it. You didn't get to be in the club unless you could afford the best of everything. Since their gear had been trashed, she had been suspecting that Seth might have more equipment than the rest of the band knew about, but it was awkward to ask. Talking about money and nice things was difficult, especially when you didn't have anything.

After a couple of days, she'd broken down and asked if he'd had one she could use, and he'd admitted he did.

Lori didn't understand why he'd held that truth so close to his vest. They were all in this together, weren't they?

Once he'd told her she could borrow it, he'd invited her over and given her his address. She recognized it immediately as one of the streets from Candle Hill, the gated neighborhood where the small minority of the town's wealthy families lived. Candle Hill was infamous for its mansions that stood behind sprawling, perfect emerald lawns.

Infamous. Lori snorted a laugh to herself as she drove her mom's old white Toyota pickup out to Seth's. Like anything could be infamous around here. The power steering was out on the truck, and Lori had to lean to the side with each turn, putting the full weight of her body behind the wheel.

Finally, she made it to his house, wrenching the wheel to make the sharp turn up his long driveway. The house was even bigger than she'd imagined it to be. It was an all-white southern colonial with white columns and a big, wrap-around porch. Though it was a newer home, it looked to Lori like what they called a plantation house in her history books. As if whoever had it built in the last twenty years set out to imbue it with the image of old wealth and power.

Lori hated it.

As she neared the driveway, she saw Seth standing next to his van, waiting with an amp by his side. He was wearing short white tennis shorts and a sleeveless shirt with The Police on it. Lori thought The Police were pretty dorky, but had to admit that he looked good with his tanned, muscular arms and legs showing off in the sun. He had a vitality that most skinny grunge boys didn't. Not unlike how she remembered Blake back when they were together, but it looked better on Seth.

Lori was glad she'd taken a little extra time with her wardrobe, even while reminding herself that it was silly, that Seth was off limits. She'd put on a short, plaid skirt, torn fishnets with black combat boots, and an extra-large Creem Magazine shirt that she'd tied up to reveal just a hint of her tummy.

She pulled the Toyota to a stop and threw on the parking brake. If she didn't, the chances of the pickup giving out and rolling back down his driveway were pretty good.

He waved at her with a beaming smile. She waved back as she walked up to him. She felt like the house was looming over her and was self-conscious in its shadow.

"You could see this house from space, Seth," she said.

"I know. It's pretty over the top," he said sheepishly.

"I can't believe they let me through the gates of Candle Hill," Lori said, self-deprecatingly.

A strange look flickered over Seth's face at her comment, but he said nothing. Lori wanted to move on. She gave him a high five for some reason, which felt awkward, then knelt in front of the amp to examine it. It was nice. A Marshall-brand practice amp. Nothing overly fancy, yet still of high quality. She could absolutely blow the roof off her little trailer with it.

"Thanks for letting me borrow this."

"Yeah, of course. Sorry, I didn't offer it, I just—I don't know, I wasn't thinking, I guess."

Lori looked into the depths of the open garage. It was clean, but smelled faintly of dust and motor oil.

It made her think of hanging out with her dad at the automotive garage. She smiled to herself.

On the far end of the garage was a wall of tools, all well-maintained. Nicer stuff than her dad had had to work with. There was a car of some kind, covered with a fitted blue tarp. She couldn't tell what it was exactly, but the vague body shape suggested some kind of sports car. Near the back, there was a door leading into the house and a stairwell going up to a room above the garage. The door was cracked open.

"Is that your room?" She pointed up the stairs.

"No, that's, *uh*," Seth stammered. His eyes darted toward the stairs and then back to her. "Just a guest room."

She knew he was hiding something from her, and she didn't like it.

"Just a guest room? Then why'd you say it like it's your serial killer hideout?"

Seth forced a laugh. "You're crazy, Lori."

Lori didn't know why she did it. Maybe it was the way he seemed to be ducking the question, maybe she just wanted to see how rich people lived, maybe it was just an impulse. Whatever the reason, she ran past Seth and up the stairs. She bolted up them, taking them two at a time, ignoring the protests he called out after her.

When she got to the top of the steps, she threw the door open and saw what Seth was hiding up there, and her mouth fell open in shock.

Chapter 9

Seth had a full studio setup. A drum kit and keyboard stood at opposite ends of the room. A 12-track Tascam recording system sat on a long table against one wall while multiple guitars and basses hung from hooks on the other.

Seth appeared behind Lori, startling her. She jumped and whirled around. He was out of breath and red-faced. He only held her attention for a second before she turned back to his setup.

Not waiting for an invitation, Lori walked into the room and soaked it all in. She couldn't believe her eyes. He had everything needed to record a full album.

"Dude, this is . . . this is *epic*. How could you not tell me you had all this stuff?"

"I was going to and then, I don't know, I felt weird about it, sort of, and then it seemed too late. I thought maybe when we were ready to record something I would tell you guys then. Like a surprise."

"But you've been using it, I'm sure," she said, running her fingers over a gorgeous 1960s Hofner viola bass hanging from the wall.

"I, *uh* . . ."

Lori turned to him, hands on hips, head cocked at a curious angle. She didn't have to say anything. He understood.

"Believe me, you don't want to hear what I've been recording," he said.

"I do!" she insisted.

"No, it's *really* not ready for anyone to hear it . . ."

"I'm not leaving this room until you play it for me," Lori said with a devilish twinkle in her eye.

Seth knew that she was telling the truth. He had no choice. "Fine . . . Come over to the Tascam."

There were two leather rolling chairs. Lori took the one off to the side and Seth sat in the chair positioned at the center of the board. He booted up the desktop computer and it whirred to life. A few minutes of loading time later, and he had the recording software up.

Lori had read about this kind of thing in *Guitar World*, but never seen it in real life. She was floored.

Seth clicked his tongue and fretted with the mouse while trying to decide what to play. Finally, he settled the cursor over a file labeled "BeautifulDay.MID".

"You promise you won't make fun of me?" he asked.

It broke her heart a little to see him so vulnerable. He really cares what I think. She suddenly felt bad for insisting he play her something. But not bad enough to extinguish her curiosity. Maybe he was hiding some hidden talent that could push Crying Lilacs even further. She had to hear it.

"I promise," she said.

He clicked the file, and a song began to play over the speakers.

Upbeat synth and drums. A hooky, melodic guitar riff. Then a voice came in. Unmistakably Seth's. Not great, but not bad. *Maybe he could do backing vocals for us*, Lori thought.

There was no irony in his lyrics. The song was, from what she could tell, quite literally about a beautiful day.

She couldn't believe it. It was so... poppy. Like Hall and Oates or something. It was profoundly... *uncool*.

"*Oh god*, you hate it," he said. He hit pause, and the song stopped.

"I don't hate it," Lori said, but she didn't tell him to keep playing. "It's just a little surprising."

"It's my side thing. Just me messing around. Being a dork, I guess."

Lori searched for something nice to say about the music, but couldn't find anything beyond it being generally competent.

Then they sat there in silence for a moment. Neither one of them knew what to do with their hands. It was the first uncomfortable quiet that they'd ever shared together, and they weren't sure what to do about it.

It was Seth who finally broke the silence. "Come here, there's something I want to show you. You're gonna like it, I promise."

Without another word, he turned and started to trot down the stairs leading to the garage.

"Wait, w-where are we going?" Lori asked, watching him leave.

He didn't turn around as he said, "It's a surprise."

Lori didn't care for surprises. In her experience,

it was rare that they were ever good. But she could hear the smile on his lips, and she knew that he was telling her the truth. She followed him.

Together they tramped down the stairs, through the garage, and into the house proper. As Lori followed him, she tried to hide how impressed she was with his family's wealth and experience.

They walked down a hallway with plush white carpet. The walls were lined with photos of a tall, good-looking man that Lori took to be Seth's father. He was posing with other important men, smiling on golf courses and in front of American flags. One of the men Lori thought might be a North Carolinian senator or congressman or something, but she couldn't be sure.

"Is that my son?" a voice called out.

Lori immediately recognized it as Julie.

Seth looked back and rolled his eyes, then led her off the hallway toward the sound of his mother's voice.

Lori followed him into a kitchen that looked straight from the pages of *Better Homes and Gardens*. All top-of-the-line appliances and fresh new tiling. Lori couldn't remember the last time she'd been in a kitchen that didn't have linoleum floors.

Julie had her back to them when they entered, but spun around to greet them. She had a broad smile on her face, just like her son's. She held a bowl of what looked to Lori like chocolate chip cookie dough that she was vigorously mixing with a wooden spoon. She wore a spotless, floral apron.

She's like a 1950s ad mom; a cartoon character. She's a Leave it to Beaver *mom.*

"Lori!" Julie exclaimed. "It is so, *so* nice to see you!" She moved toward Lori, then remembered the bowl in her arms. "*Oops!* Silly me. Let me put this down."

Julie set the bowl on the marble counter, then stepped forward and wrapped Lori in a big, uninvited hug. Lori knew she should feel welcomed and warm, but she didn't. Instead, she felt a strange, burning anger in her gut. She didn't know why, and it confused her.

Still, she lightly hugged Julie back, patting her. Julie stepped away and assessed her. "You are so darn pretty, I swear!"

She snatched Seth up in a similar hug, as he made eye contact with Lori and mouthed the words, "I'm sorry."

Finally, Julie released him, stepped back, and said, "Do you kids need snacks? Juice, water? There's soda, but it's so bad for you. Maybe some Crystal Pepsi? I think that's less sugar."

Watching Julie fawn over her son, Lori realized what the hot, churning feeling in her guts was. Jealousy. Seth didn't just have a mom, he had a mother. For all that Lori's mom did for her, she might as well have been living on her own.

She couldn't stand being in that perfect kitchen with them. She had to get out.

"Weren't you gonna show me something, Seth?" she said, interrupting Julie.

"*Oh* yeah, come on," Seth said and started leading her back to the hallway. Over his shoulder, he said, "Thanks, Mom, but we're good. Love you."

As Lori followed him out, she heard Julie call out behind them, "Love you too, baby!"

Seth took Lori down the hall to a large foyer where a crystal chandelier hung high over their heads. They went up the stairs covered in the same thick, white carpeting. When they reached the landing overlooking the foyer, Seth took a left. They walked past multiple heavy wooden doors, all closed.

Lori wondered if she tested the handles, would they be locked? Did rich people lock their doors?

At the end of the hall, Seth led her up another flight of stairs. *Jeez, this house doesn't end,* Lori thought. The stairs brought them to a landing bathed in sunlight from multiple wide windows. There was only one door. He pushed it open, and they walked into what she immediately knew was his bedroom. The walls were covered in posters of pop stars. No legitimate rockers, unlike in Lori's bedroom. Seth's posters weren't like any other kid's she'd seen. They were in frames.

On the table beside his raised four-poster bed, there was a phone made of see-through plastic so that the guts of the machine were visible.

"Cool phone," Lori said.

"Thanks." He walked past his bed to a large window on the far wall. He pushed the window open and turned to her with a grin. "After you," he said.

"What?" Lori asked. She didn't know what else to say.

"Relax," he laughed. "It leads out onto the roof."

She went to the window and stuck her head out. Sure enough, the roof was right underneath. She hiked her leg over the sill and stepped out onto the shingled surface. She was looking out at the world behind Seth's house. Nothing but trees and nature. The sun was warm, and the breeze carried the scent of freshly cut grass.

Seth stepped up next to her. "Follow me," he said and began walking toward the edge of the roof, which had a subtle slope downward.

Lori followed. The closer they got to the edge, the more the landscape behind the house revealed itself to her.

"There. That's what I wanted to show you. This was the inspiration for the song."

He didn't need to say anything; Lori would have stopped in her tracks all on her own.

Right behind Seth's house, practically in his backyard, was a perfect, crystal clear lake. The surface shimmered in the sun. Ducks floated about and happily quacked. It was absolutely beautiful and serene.

Things might not be so nice back home in her own life, but here up on Seth's roof, it was indeed a beautiful day.

Drawn by the beauty of the lake, Lori took another step forward, right to the edge of the roof. Her eyes were locked on it, so she didn't look back at Seth when she said, "Thank you for sharing this with me."

She was grinning to herself when her feet suddenly went out from under her, and she fell over the edge.

Chapter 10

Lori was free-falling.

Her body was toppling over the edge of a thirty-foot drop down to the earth.

She closed her eyes and prepared for death.

Then strong arms were wrapping around her and stopping her descent. *Seth*.

For a moment, she hung there, suspended in midair. She opened her eyes and looked down. The ground was so far away.

She gasped as Seth pulled her back onto the roof, practically dragging her away from the edge. Her heart was beating out of her chest, and she couldn't catch her breath. He put his hands on her shoulders to steady her.

"It's okay. You're going to be okay," Seth said, looking into her eyes.

Lori couldn't figure out how she had fallen. She was close to the edge, sure, but she'd been on solid ground. She looked back to where she'd fallen and noticed a loose shingle. It had come free and slipped.

"The shingle," Lori said between deep breaths. "It must have come out from under me."

"I'm so sorry! I'll tell my dad, and we'll get that

fixed right away. Lori, I never would have brought you up here if I didn't think it was safe."

"You-you saved me."

She looked up at Seth, and, for just a moment, she felt like she was in a movie. One of those cheesy movies she hated, the kind her mom liked to watch when she was just the right amount of wine-drunk, where a boy meets a girl, and they kiss, and the cameras spin all around them, and they get a house together or whatever. They made her want to puke. But for just a second, it felt nice to feel like she might have been cast in a starring role.

Romances are bad for the band. The words played out loud and clear in the back of her mind. She shook off the excitement that had gripped her for a moment. *So lame*, she thought. She didn't really want that anyway. *Right?*

"Let's go inside," she said, stepping back from him while keeping an eye on the edge of the roof.

"Yeah, totally," Seth agreed.

He led her back to the window, and they climbed through into the quiet stillness of his bedroom.

After a few seconds, Seth broke the silence. "Lori, I'm sorry I didn't tell you about the recording stuff and gear and all. To be totally honest with you, I just didn't want you guys to look at me differently. You know, like this rich kid who had lessons and all these nice instruments. I know I'm talented, and I believe in myself, but . . . people don't take you seriously. They think the ability to play was given to you."

Lori didn't say it, but she wondered if she'd be better than she was if she'd had lessons beyond her dad teaching her some power chords.

"You're so talented, and without all or, you know, some of my luck, you know? It's sort of embarrassing."

He looked so sad, she really felt for him then. Everybody had problems, no matter where they came from. Seth was proof of that. He was also right. It was a bit hard not to think of him differently after seeing all that he had, and she didn't. Still, different didn't mean bad. Seth's dad might be some corporate scumbag, but it wasn't a reason to judge him.

Lori smiled at him reassuringly. "You know we wouldn't drag you like that, dude. You play with your heart. That's what matters. You can bring any crappy piece of gear, or you can come jam with a classic Les Paul, as long as you play with your heart. And you do."

"Thanks, Lori. Really, that means a lot. I know you guys wouldn't judge me." A smile slowly spread across his face. He half-whispered, like he was telling a secret. "Also, part of it is that my mom doesn't like me loaning out my gear."

Lori broke into laughter and punched him in the shoulder. "You are such a mama's boy!"

He playfully gave her a shove, but didn't protest her assessment of him. They both knew it was true.

"Does she think your trashy friend is gonna pawn your amp for junk?"

Seth's expression went suddenly serious. Almost fierce. "Hey. Don't talk about yourself like that, Lori. You're not trash. You shouldn't say things like that."

Lori felt embarrassed but couldn't pinpoint why. After all, she'd made the joke herself.

"I was just kidding around," she said, hoping she didn't sound as defensive as she thought.

"I know, it just . . . it bums me out to hear you talk about yourself like that."

"I should probably go," Lori said, even though she didn't want to. "It's getting late, and I have to help my mom with dinner."

"All right, I'll walk you down to your truck."

She followed Seth back down through the house, past all the expensive furnishings and photos with famous-looking people. She breathed a sigh of relief when they went by the kitchen and didn't get hassled by Julie. The kitchen was empty, filled only with the smell of baking chocolate chip cookies.

She found Julie when they passed by the living room. The super mom was in front of the TV, going crazy on a NordicTrack. The TV was playing the news on mute while she listened to headphones connected to a Walkman. She had a look of absolute determination on her face and was covered in sweat. She looked like she'd been going for a while.

The woman is intense, I'll give her that, thought Lori. She was dying to know what music Julie worked out to. Probably Yanni.

As soon as they entered the garage, Lori made a beeline for the amp. She was so focused on how it would play, wondering how high she could get the gain up, she didn't even notice her car.

"Lori, stop! Your truck . . ."

She turned to Seth first and saw his look of utter shock. Then she looked at the Toyota. From the hood to the tailgate, its white surface was covered in horrible words, crudely written in crimson red.

Freak. Slut. Loser. No talent. The words popped out at her, taunting her. Then she read the one that really hurt her: *Crying Lilacs SUX*.

Inside, she was crushed, but she didn't want to let on. She wanted Seth to think she was tough. A leader. But tears welled in her eyes. She couldn't help it.

"Who would do this?" she asked.

When he spoke, Seth's voice was shaky. Frightened. "That's not paint, Lori. That's blood."

Chapter 11

Blood? Could it really be blood? So many messages covered the car that it would have taken at least a gallon . . .

"Seth, I don't think that's what it is," Lori said.

The deep crimson letters dripped down the sides of the truck. It did look an awful lot like blood. Was she trying to convince Seth or herself that it wasn't?

She scanned the landscape past the garage. The yard and street beyond were empty. Whoever had done this had snuck up and then gotten away quickly, she decided. At least she and Seth were safe.

Lori approached the truck slowly, tentatively, as if the words themselves might jump out and grab her. She stopped at the hood of the car and looked down at the word emblazoned there: FREAK. So red and angry. Lori ran her fingers along the letter F. Whatever substance had been used to write the word was so fresh it was still drying. It felt tacky on her skin. She pulled her finger back to find a little bit of red sticking to the subtle ridges of her fingertip. Raising her finger to her nose, she took a sniff.

Relief flooded her body. It was the unmistakable scent of paint. Just paint. The harassment was still horrible, still frightening, but at least it wasn't blood. Lori turned back to Seth and forced a grin, desperate to hide her true feelings and show she was above all of this.

"Some creep just tagged it with spray paint. No blood."

Seth still looked twisted up with worry. "I . . . I can't believe this. Why are they doing this to you? To us?" He looked nervously around the garage, as if someone might still be lurking somewhere inside. "They came to my house . . . Wait a minute. How did they know you were here?"

He had a good point. Lori realized then that someone was following her. *Stalking* her. If it didn't stop at the destruction of their instruments, she knew that it wouldn't stop after this. Whoever was doing this wanted Crying Lilacs to go away. She had to be vigilant, on the lookout for her stalker from this point forward.

Whoever this was, she could handle. She would figure it out and stop them. She had to.

"Whoever it is, they're messing with the wrong person," Lori said.

"It's all cool until someone gets hurt." Seth's voice trembled with worry. "I mean it. This is really crazy. I don't get why you're not totally freaking out right now."

"Honestly, I'm way more worried about what my mom is going to say about the truck."

Seth walked out of the garage, and the sun illuminated his tan skin and bold shock of black hair. He came in close and looked like he was going to hug Lori, and as badly as she wanted it, she couldn't accept it. As much as she needed a little reassurance and care at that moment, she knew that if she were wrapped in the embrace of a friend, she might just break like a dam and cry, and she couldn't let it out. She couldn't show that weakness. Seth wasn't as strong as she was, and it would make him worry even more. That fear would reverberate through the whole band, and she had to keep them together no matter what.

Seth began to open his arms, and Lori took a step back, pretending to turn her attention back toward the word painted on the hood of the truck. Seth awkwardly lowered his arms.

"It's going to be okay. She can't be mad at you, it's not your fault."

An image of Julie hugging Seth flashed in Lori's mind.

"*Oh*, Seth, it doesn't matter if it's my fault or not. She's gonna kill me."

"I'm gonna kill you!" Amber shrieked from the trailer doorway. She marched down the rickety wooden steps leading down to the ground and headed straight for Lori, fists clenched. She leaned in toward Lori, and the fumes of cheap vodka wafted into her daughter's face as she yelled, "What the hell happened to the car? This is disgusting!"

"Somebody tagged the car, Mom. Why are you getting mad at me? Like I did this?" Lori spoke through gritted teeth. Lori tried not to raise her voice, but it was difficult to control herself when she was being punished for something she didn't do. She didn't want things to escalate, which they always did when her mom was drinking.

"*Oh*, you didn't do it? You didn't make someone angry by acting like a wild animal in that band?" Her mom pointed at the words CRYING LILACS SUX spray-painted across the side of the truck bed.

"You can't blame me for that! Who cares anyway? I'm not gonna be ashamed of what this stupid little town thinks of me. I'll drive it no matter what."

"If you drive around in that car like that, you're going to show them that you're just as trashy as they think you are."

The comment was like a punch to the face. Lori had been called every name in the book by the people of this town, and her mother had yelled at her plenty of times in frustration, but it was always about dumb things like picking up her room. She'd never attacked her character before. Lori was so hurt, so stunned, that she didn't even know what to say.

"I'm outta here."

As she turned to get back in the truck, her mother grabbed her by the arm. The bony fingers clenching around her wrist felt just like the zombified hands from her nightmare in sex ed. Shivers ran up her arm, emanating from Amber's fingertips, and an image flashed in her mind of the undead gripping, pulling, and dragging her down. Down to hell.

"Wait, please," Amber said.

Lori stopped, turned. The anger had dissipated from her mother's face, and in its place was a look of profound pain. A look Lori hadn't seen since the death of her father. Was she grieving again? For the fear of losing a daughter?

"I'm sorry." Her mother's voice was barely a whisper. "Maybe . . . maybe the guys at your dad's old shop will help us out. Maybe they can get the paint off somehow. For free."

Lori wanted to hug her mother, then. To apologize for snapping and promise she would get it fixed up and be a better daughter, be whatever she wanted. But she couldn't. One pitiful look didn't erase the years of damage she'd done. It didn't undo the fact that she'd revealed she looked down upon her own daughter just as much as the other adults in town.

She yanked her arm from her mom's grasp. She got back in the truck, gunned the motor, and drove away, leaving the drunk woman standing alone in front of the trailer.

The scene with her mother played over and over as she pulled into the parking lot at school the next day. She had spent the night before sleeping in the bed of the truck on an old blanket she got from the rehearsal barn. It had been peaceful sleeping under the stars, but she was very aware that her clothes were rumpled and dirty, and she had a bit of a rank odor exuding from them.

As soon as she entered the school's lot, she could feel the eyes of every kid out there turn to her. They pointed and stared at the cruel words on the truck. Some of them laughed. Some of them looked at her with pity, which was worse. Some just stared in open-mouthed shock.

Lori didn't care. Let them stare. *Screw 'em.* She smiled back at them all and waved like a beauty queen in a parade.

She was looking for a spot when she saw Meadow and Memphis waving at her from the hood of Meadow's old Buick. She pulled over to the spot next to them, cut the engine, and applied the truck's parking brake.

The duo was on her with a flurry of questions before she'd barely even gotten out of the truck.

"What happened?" / "Are you okay?" / "Who did this?" / "What did your mom say?"

Lori tried to answer each question in order, but Meadow squeezed her in a hug so tight that the air was pushed out of her lungs.

When she finally let her go, Lori said, "I didn't see who did it. Somebody is following me. They tagged me at Seth's house." Meadow gave her a knowing side-eye, and Lori clarified, "I was there to borrow an amp."

"Man . . ." Memphis ran a finger over the L in the word LOSER painted along the rim of her back tire. "This is high-quality spray paint. Lawson brand, *Cherry Red*."

The girls stared at him for a long moment. "I used to tag stuff, okay? It was a long time ago! I was just a kid, but I got really into it."

"Yeah, I'm sure you never huffed any of it," Meadow teased.

"Man, whatever. But yeah, this is good stuff."

Lawson brand, Cherry Red. Lori repeated the line over and over in her head. It wasn't much info, but it was a clue.

"Okay, so ignoring Memphis' childhood addiction

to huffing spray paint for a moment, Seth had an extra amp just lying around?" Meadow asked.

"Yeah, he had an extra. No big deal."

"How about an extra bass? I don't know how you fixed the Jaguar, but mine is trashed."

"Yeah, my kit is KIA too," Memphis interjected.

For a moment, she considered telling the two about Seth's setup, but decided to keep it to herself. It wasn't hers to share. He could tell them when he was ready. Besides, she figured that this could be a galvanizing moment for the band. Overcoming challenges brought people together.

"Sorry, guys, no free drums and bass lying around. We can figure this out, though. We've still got a week and a half until the Battle."

The three of them stood in silence for a moment in the parking lot, kicking at the gravel and passing around a cigarette, the last one from Memphis' pack. Finally, Meadow's face brightened.

"Guys, I have an idea!"

Chapter 12

The crashing sounds of bowling pins echoed back into the walk-in janitor's closet. Meadow stared into the cracked mirror, little more than a shard that hung over a grimy, paint-stained sink, at Lori, who stood behind her.

"Some green room," Meadow quipped.

Lori shrugged. "It's Bowl-o-rama, not Max's Kansas City," she said over the clattering call of more pins being knocked down. "Pretty cool they let us play on such short notice."

Lori felt anxious and trapped in the closet. She chewed nervously at her bottom lip. It was a huge night. The culmination of the big idea Meadow had had in the school parking lot only the day before.

They were having a fundraising show. Their opportunity to get enough cash to replace their broken instruments.

She wasn't worried about getting instruments to play for the fundraiser itself. Their school's jazz band had loaned them what they needed, but the instruments were in bad shape. It was a temporary solution. If they were going to win, they needed the best gear they could get that could capture the tone of their music and take a beating on stage.

What worried Lori was that they had put everything into the show. It was the only way they could make enough money in time to play the Battle of the Bands. And even if they didn't raise enough and could play on Seth's instruments, it was proof that the community didn't care about them.

The way Lori figured it, if people didn't show up for this, they wouldn't show up and vote for them to win at the battle.

The fundraising show *had* to work.

"Let's play so loud we shatter every piece of glass in the place and make 'em regret it." Meadow delicately brushed on neon pink eye shadow, creating a sharp, angular point. "Hey," she stopped and turned to Lori. "Do you think I should shave my head? Or go crew cut? I wanna go like, *butch*, dude. But then, like, super girly makeup and stuff. It's a statement." When Lori didn't reply and instead stared worriedly off into space, Meadow smiled and said, "Okay, no problem, I'm almost done. I'm gonna get out of here so you can do your little ritual."

"Sorry, Mead. It's not that. It's just..." Lori chewed on her lip. "What if nobody comes?"

A fist pounded against the door, and Lori jumped.

"It's time, you two." Seth's voice came through the door. He sounded downbeat, which made Lori's stomach sink.

"One sec," Meadow replied. She approached her friend and ran her hand down Lori's arms, comforting her, then wrapped her in a hug. "Lori, we did everything we could. We told everyone we knew. We posted flyers all over town. You know it better than anyone, we can't control whether people like us or show up for us. If we're going to be failed by other people again, it's okay. 'Cause we're here with each other. Right?"

Lori could feel that the question wasn't rhetorical. As much as Meadow was working to console her, she needed to have the question answered for herself as well.

"Right," Lori whispered back.

Meadow dropped the hug and pulled the door open to reveal Seth standing there with a hangdog look on his face.

"*Oh* no," Lori said, and Seth didn't refute it.

"We've got to play the show no matter how big the audience is," he said.

He turned and walked away toward the party room of the bowling alley, a rundown room with stained carpets and scuffed walls where little kids had their birthday parties. Lori and Meadow followed behind, heads hung like two outlaws being led to the gallows.

The party room, as they approached, sounded empty and looked dark. *God*, Lori thought, *is it completely dead in there?* When they stepped inside, Seth reached out and flicked a light switch on the wall, and the fluorescent ceiling lights flickered to life, revealing a room absolutely packed with people who all let out a cheer for their arrival.

Lori was stunned. She looked around the room at the smiling faces, the people all standing shoulder to shoulder, crammed in the little room that smelled like old popcorn and sweat, and she thought she might break down crying. The crowd consisted of kids from Roosevelt High, new faces, townies, and even a few musicians from rival bands.

Any one of them could have been the person in the barn, Lori thought for a second, then pushed it from her mind.

Lori whirled on Seth, her expression a jumble of relief and elation, shock and annoyance.

Seth gave her a boyish, mischievous smirk. "I asked them all to be quiet and surprise you."

Lori slapped his arm and cried out, "You jerk!" but she couldn't have been feeling more differently about him at that moment.

"Let's go!" a voice cried out over the crowd.

Lori looked to the stage where Memphis was standing behind his kit, drumsticks raised triumphantly in the air. Lori had never seen him so confident and happy. His long hair was pulled back into a sloppy ponytail to show his face, and his normally sloping shoulders were held a little higher than normal.

Lori began to push through the crowd, leading the way for Seth and Meadow. Hands slapped their backs as they went.

Suddenly, someone grabbed Lori's arm.

She turned to find an older man in the crowd. He had a crew cut and was dressed conservatively in a polo shirt and crisp blue jeans. He was wiry, yet muscular. Sweat poured down his forehead. His eyes contained an intensity that made Lori immediately uncomfortable.

"You guys are the best! You're gonna rock tonight!" he gushed.

"Totally. Thanks, man," Lori said.

She pulled her arm from his grasp and moved on

through the crowd. Behind her, she heard Meadow say, loud enough for the man to hear, "Wow, I didn't know undercover cops were into our shows," and Lori snickered to herself.

They made it to the small, rickety stage in the back of the room that was usually reserved for birthday clowns and magicians. Lori clambered up, then offered a hand to Meadow and Seth. She grinned at Memphis, and he returned it.

The band took their positions on the stage. Lori looked to the other side of the party room, where a bored, chubby bald man sat behind a little table with the lighting and sound equipment. She gave the man a thumbs-up. He shrugged.

The room lights went down while the stage lights went up.

"Thank you so much," Lori said into the microphone. "With your ticket sales and donations, we'll be able to battle and *win*."

The crowd cheered, and Lori played the opening notes to their song "Black Star," and the rest of the band fell in behind her.

She hadn't been able to repair the Jaguar as well as she'd thought, and it was falling out of tune by the middle of the song. Memphis' drum kit from the school didn't sound great either, but he was in perfect time.

Just as they reached a wailing crescendo toward the end of "Black Star," Lori looked out over the crowd. Faces grinned up at her. The strange, older man from earlier was nowhere to be seen . . .

Then she saw it. A masked face amidst the crowd.

While others pogoed or pumped their fists to the

rhythm of the song, the figure stood stock still amidst the chaos, staring straight ahead, clad in a black hooded robe.

A horrible void stared back at her.

She knew it was impossible over the din of the music and the crowd, but she swore that for a moment she heard the attacker's heavy breathing reverberating inside her skull.

Lori lost her place in the song; the lyrics caught in her throat. Her hands froze. She fumbled a chord, and Seth covered it up with a quick run of improvised lead notes.

A stage light flared in her vision and blinded her. She winced and pulled away from the mic. Shaking her head, she blinked like mad and fought the stars out of her vision.

When she looked back out into the crowd, the figure was gone.

Chapter 13

Meadow fanned the money out in her hand and waved it in her face, enjoying the self-created breeze. Fives and tens and twenties rippled through the air.

"Money, money, money!" she said in a sing-song voice. "Man, a lot of those kids used to treat us like crap, but I gotta say, they really showed up for us tonight. Maybe this town isn't so bad after all."

"They like you after you prove you have value to them. We're doing something cool, and we're doing it well. They just want something from us," Lori said.

As she watched her friend, bathed in the full moon hanging over the parking lot, she tried to count the money flapping in her hands but lost count.

Meadow smirked at her. "What, to bask in our glory? Somebody's conceited."

"No, I didn't mean it like that, Mead. It's . . . you know how it is—ugly duckling syndrome. I appreciate the money, I do, but what matters most is how you treat the little duck when it's still ugly. It's like—"

"I get it. Your feelings on the matter are complicated. Forget about all that, just look at this *money*."

Meadow had folded the cash up into a thick green

brick and slapped it against her palm. It let out a satisfying *thwack*.

Lori looked nervously around the loading dock of the bowling alley. Cracked pavement and graffiti. The place was rundown and, except for the noise of the patrons echoing out from inside, totally silent. A single fluorescent light hanging over the back door of the venue flickered on and off. The spot gave Lori the creeps.

The money, combined with their open van full of instruments and amps, was begging to be stolen. One more opportunity for the scumbag behind the mask who had been watching them.

"You shouldn't wave it around like that. You're going to get us robbed."

Meadow's grin fell away. Sulkily, she handed the thick wad of cash to Lori.

"Fine, *Mom*," she said, as Lori took the money and wedged it into her pocket.

She'd taken the wind out of her friend's sails, and she felt bad, but knew that she was right. Of course, Meadow didn't know that there had been someone out there in the crowd. Someone who could be anywhere at that moment.

"Sorry, Meadow. I'm just on edge 'cause . . ."

She trailed off. She didn't want to unnecessarily frighten Meadow, but at the same time, her friend deserved to know. She wanted to tell Seth, too, but he was inside talking with some guys she didn't recognize after the show.

"What? You can tell me," Meadow said softly, dropping the edge in her voice.

"I saw him. In the crowd. The masked guy who

trashed our gear and tried to attack me. Or did, I guess, just not very well."

"What?!" Meadow's voice went up two octaves, and her eyes darted about, searching the inky night surrounding them.

"He was in the crowd and then he . . . wasn't. He just vanished. Great story, I know."

"Where's Blake?" Meadow demanded.

"*Huh?* How should I know?"

"I mean, we should check the parking lot. Maybe his dumb car is out there, or, *oh*, wait! What about that guy?"

"What guy?" Lori asked.

"The old weird guy, the crew cut guy that grabbed you."

Of course. *That* guy.

"Maybe?" Lori answered. "I didn't see him at the same time I saw the masked dude, but he could've just been off grabbing a soda."

"Or like, taking a dump," Memphis said, rounding the side of the van in a slow, loping gait. He laughed to himself and said dreamily, "Sorry, I don't even know what you guys are talking about."

The drummer had been sitting up in the front of the van. Lori hadn't questioned why, and, as she smelled the weed wafting off of him, she didn't have to.

"You played good tonight, dude." She high-fived him.

"Really?" Memphis asked, blushing.

"Yeah, man! I could tell you'd been practicing. You were tight up there."

Memphis held his hands up. They were covered in raw, angry blisters where he'd been holding his drumsticks, pounding the skins for hours at a time. She'd never been more grateful to him. Memphis wasn't the most naturally talented drummer in the world, but it didn't matter. There were plenty of people for whom talent came easily, but it didn't mean a thing because they weren't willing to work for it. Memphis gave it his all, even when it caused him physical pain.

Lori was about to ask if he needed bandages or something for his hands when the sudden *blat* of a car horn startled her and pulled her attention to the two-lane blacktop running behind the bowling alley. A jacked-up pickup truck, a big red Ford, was racing down the empty road. Its horn bleated obnoxiously into the night for no reason other than to annoy anyone in earshot. Two big Confederate flags hung from poles mounted on the rear bumper and flapped in the wind.

Lori cringed inside. *It won't be long now,* she told herself. *You'll get away, and this place will all be a memory.*

Then the light went out.

It had been flickering irregularly the whole time they'd been packing out and talking on the loading dock, but this time, it didn't come back on, and they were cast into darkness. Total, silent darkness.

Lori's stomach knotted up with dread. She pressed her finger to her lips and gave Memphis and Meadow hard, urgent looks. *Keep still. Keep silent.*

She turned away from her friends and looked at the dead light hanging over the door. The bulb hadn't been broken. Had someone loosened it? Cut the electrical cord? She scanned the surrounding area, looking for any sudden movement in the darkness, listening for an advancing footstep in the quiet night.

She was peering at the nearest corner of the bowling alley when the light, for just a moment, flickered back to life and illuminated something peeking from behind the wall.

The face. The black, featureless nothing.

Then the light died, and the face melted back into the night.

Without hesitating, Lori yanked the van's keys from her pocket and tossed them to Meadow.

"Both of you get in the van and lock the doors," she hissed to her friends.

"Wait, Lori, wha—" Meadow stammered in protest.

But Lori was already running toward the corner, pursuing the monster in the dark.

Chapter 14

By the time Lori reached the corner, the masked figure was already halfway to the other side of the bowling alley, running alongside the decaying brick wall of the building. The man, at least Lori thought they were a man, was going at a full-on sprint and had quite a bit of speed. His black cloak fluttered behind him.

"Great, he's an Olympian," Lori muttered to herself.

She took off after him, running as hard and as fast as she could, picking her feet up over the beer bottles and fast food bags littering the ground. She was already winded by the time she'd reached the midpoint between the first corner and the second. She breathed deep and ran harder, fighting through the burning sensation rising in her lungs and legs.

She kept her eyes on the figure and didn't see the two-liter bottle of Mello Yello until she was stepping on it. Her ankle rolled out from under her, and she dropped to the ground. Skin tore away from her knees as she landed in the rocky dirt. She winced, sucking in a sharp gulp of air, but there was no time for pain.

Lori clambered to her feet, looking up for the masked man, but he was nowhere to be seen.

He hadn't veered left and taken off across the empty lot next to the bowling alley. As fast as he was, she would have still been able to see him. No, he had to have gone around the opposite corner of the building.

Brushing the dirt off as she went, she hustled after him until she reached the corner. There, she stopped, pressing herself against the rough brick wall. Took a deep breath. Careful not to reveal herself around the corner, she listened. She heard voices from the entrance of the bowling alley. Kids standing around outside smoking and jawing. She heard running footsteps and shouted goodbyes and cars honking as people got in their cars and pulled out of the parking lot. She did not hear the masked man.

But what would those sounds even be? A knife being sharpened? A shotgun cocking? Maniacal laughter? What sounds can one expect from a silent psycho?

One thing she definitely didn't hear was reactions from anyone out front. If a masked madman had run into her while she was smoking a clove and talking to a friend in front of Bowl-o-rama, Lori would have something to say about it.

There was only one way for her to find the guy, if he was even still out there. She couldn't prepare. She couldn't get the drop on him. She had to step out into the light and let him come to her.

Easier said than done. She took a deep breath and turned around the corner, fists raised like every boxer she'd ever seen on TV, and came face to face with—

"Blake?" Her voice came out higher, more frightened, than she'd wanted, and she was embarrassed.

"*Oh*, hey, babe." Blake smirked down at her.

A sheen of sweat covered his forehead. Just like he'd been running... But he wasn't out of breath... Lori scanned his outfit. Black cargo pants, black Air Jordan high tops, a black turtleneck. She'd never seen Blake wear anything other than polo shirts and blue jeans the whole time she'd dated him. That and the self-satisfied tone in his voice told her it had to be him.

Yes, she told herself, he had whipped around the corner and then waited for her. Blake was a star athlete; he could have easily sprinted around the building without getting winded. He'd once bragged to her that he could hold his breath underwater for five whole minutes. She'd told him that would make him brain-dead. He didn't get the insult.

But if it was Blake... *Where was the mask? The billowing black cloak?*

Lori studied the scrubby bushes planted along the façade of the bowling alley to see if he'd quickly hidden the costume. *Nothing*. Just thin, dry plants struggling to hold onto life. They could barely conceal anything.

Could he have run all the way to his car and then come back? Lori doubted it. She scanned the parking lot for his Jaguar but didn't see any sign of the car.

"You're all flustered and out of breath, Lori. I guess I have that effect, *huh?*" he said smugly.

He stepped toward her, invading her space. A flash of memory reminded her how much she'd enjoyed his height when they had first started dating. He stood nearly a foot taller than her, and it excited her, made her feel like she was dating a big man inside and out. To all outside appearances, she was. The tall, blonde captain of the football team. The big quarterback. Then she'd realized how small he was inside, and his exterior mattered less and less until she couldn't see anything good about him at all.

Now, she wished his exterior matched his true character. He'd be as small as a cockroach. Perfectly sized to be squished beneath her Chuck Taylors.

"Where's your stupid little cape, Blake? You know this loser costume you have, not only is it not scary, but it's dorky as hell, too."

"What? A *cape*? What are you talking about?" Blake's voice quavered, his face twisted up in confusion.

The boy's mental capacity meant that a state of confusion was the rule, not the exception, but Lori found that he was usually pretty good at pretending to know what was up in social situations. Especially situations where he wanted to maintain power. The obvious uncertainty in his voice made Lori second-guess her conviction.

Maybe it wasn't Blake after all ...

"What are you doing here?" she demanded.

"I wanted to see your little show. You rocked it, babe. Sure you made a lotta cash, too. You know I put some in there. Fifty bucks. You find a crisp fifty bill in that wad, and you'll know it was from your man."

"Look, I can't deal with whatever this is, Blake, I . . ." Lori rubbed her temples, exasperated. The fear and adrenaline were draining from her body, and she was now just angry, annoyed that she had to waste her time and energy with him again. But how to get him to leave? Flattery, she decided. "Blake, you can have any girl you want. You know that, right?"

"I basically have," he said, puffing out his chest.

Lori had to fight not to roll her eyes.

"Right, yeah. Sure. So then, why me? What are you doing standing there every time I turn around?"

He took a step toward her. "Because I don't want any other girl. I want you." He reached out and brushed her cheek with the knuckles of his hand. Rough, cracked flesh rubbed against her face, and she flinched, pulled away. He looked offended. "You know, before all this music crap, you were a normal girl. So pretty. Nobody looked better in a little sundress than you, babe. Remember all those clothes I bought you?"

She remembered it differently. Blake was dressing her up like a doll, like his perfect little bubbly, preppy chick that he could cart around on his arm. Thinking back on that time, all those days she had allowed him to make her into something she wasn't, just so she could feel some kind of acceptance from someone *normal*, filled her with humiliation and regret.

The one thing she hadn't regretted was leaving him. The fact that it had taken him pushing her down in the mud outside of the Spring Formal in front of all his friends because she'd made him feel stupid about a book they were reading in English class wasn't ideal, but at least she'd done it. She'd gone home that night covered in mud and was determined to never look back, to make her own future and pursue her dream. Covered in mud . . . so much for the dress he'd bought her.

Lori didn't say any of this. She looked at his rough knuckles and noticed they were slightly swollen from an old bruise. Light purple, growing sickly yellow at the edges. As if he'd been in a fight. Or punching and breaking instruments . . .

If she got in his face, would he hesitate to hit her? Lori knew that it started with a shove into the mud, but would only get worse from there.

She spoke calmly, but firmly. "Blake. I don't want to be with you. I need you to leave me alone. It's that simple."

His lips creased into a deep frown before morphing into a snarl; his upper lip curled up to reveal his gleaming white teeth. He reached out as if to grab her arm and pull her toward him, but froze when he heard a voice call out down the sidewalk in front of the bowling alley.

"Lori! Hey!"

They both turned to the sound of the voice, and Lori breathed a sigh of relief.

Seth.

He jogged up with that affable grin plastered on his face and gave Blake a little wave.

"Hey, man," he said as he came to a stop next to Lori. "What's your name again?"

Nice, Lori thought. A guy like Blake didn't take well to disrespect from other men, even small slights like forgetting his name.

"What's yours?" Blake retorted. He turned to Lori and snarled, "Who is this guitar douche?"

Lori was surprised they didn't know each other.

They both lived in the same affluent neighborhood. For all of her talk about liking skinny rocker boys in torn jeans, she certainly had a type. Looking back and forth from the tall, muscular Seth to the slightly taller and even more muscular Blake, made Lori snicker.

"What's so funny?" Blake demanded.

"You, loser," Lori said, and with that, she turned and walked back around the corner of the building. Seth followed close behind. They walked for a moment in silence before Lori asked, "Is he following us?"

Seth snuck a look over his shoulder and replied, "No, all clear." Then he added, "Sorry, I wasn't around. I started talking to the bowling alley owner about vintage Gibsons. He really knows his stuff."

"It's fine. I don't need you to like, defend me. Blake's my problem. I can handle him on my own." *Why am I being so defensive?* Lori wondered. He was just being nice, like a good friend should be. Meadow or Memphis would have done the same thing. And he did help, at least with the exit. That was made much easier. Finally, she said, "Sorry, that came out weird. I appreciate it, man."

"Yeah, dude, no problem."

Hearing him call her dude made Lori feel strange. Another negative emotion she couldn't readily identify the source of. What was going on with her?

"Where are Memphis and Meadow?" Seth asked as they walked over the garbage littering their path.

"*Oh!*" Lori had totally forgotten about them in all the chaos. "They locked themselves in the van."

Seth snorted a disbelieving laugh, like she must be joking.

"I'm serious," she said.

"Why?"

"I'll explain on the ride home. But long story short, I think Blake is the one who's been sabotaging us."

Chapter 15

Sweat poured over Lori's brow, and her breath came in short, ragged gasps as she went into her fourth lap around Roosevelt High's outdoor track. Even in the spring, the humidity in North Carolina made every move feel like she was wading through the deep end of a pool. She looked behind her. Only six kids were in her wake as she rounded the bend into the final stretch of the mile-long run.

She regretted the night before with every fiber of her being. After the show and the face-off with Blake, the band met up with some friends at a house party where they drank beer, smoked weed and cigarettes, and danced and screamed to hardcore records all night long. One by one, the members of Crying Lilacs peeled off and went home, until it was just Lori and some townies who were a few years older than her watching the sun come up from the roof of the decaying old house they'd been partying in.

She staggered into school and arrived fifteen minutes late to gym class with no sleep, no water, and no food. Coach Teller had eyeballed her as she'd walked in, and she knew that, in that moment, he decided to make all of them run the mile.

Staggering and gasping for breath, Lori pulled into the finish line just behind Marty Whitehead, who had lost his left leg two years prior in a farming accident. Meadow was there waiting for her with a half-empty Gatorade.

"You wanna be like Mike?" Meadow asked. "It's Midnight Thunder flavor, and I drank half of it, but—"

It could have been yak pee for all Lori cared in that moment. She snatched it from Meadow and desperately guzzled it down, letting it pour over her chin and onto her sweat-drenched shirt.

When the bottle was drained of every drop, she wiped her mouth and gasped, "Thank you."

"When did you get home?" Meadow asked, concern rising in her voice.

"I didn't. I kept raging and then drove in here. Honestly, I'm still a little drunk, I think."

"Jeez," Meadow murmured. "Are you doing okay, Lori?"

Of course she wasn't, and the instinct to mock her friend's question rose and then flitted away. Instead, Lori said, "I'm fine. What about you?"

Before Meadow could answer, Coach Teller stomped up to them. Lori shielded her eyes from the blazing sun so she could see him properly. His angry, beet-red face was smudged with white smears of sunscreen. He gestured to the other kids sitting in the grass surrounding them, recuperating from their own runs.

"Ninety percent of these kids got in front of you, Lori," he said in his Southern drawl, his tone low and gruff.

"I finished the run, what more do you want?" Lori retorted.

The coach took in a big, exaggerated whiff through his nose. "Jesus, kid, it's a Tuesday morning. What are you doing? You reek of alcohol and tobacco."

"First the whacky weed accusation and now this? What are you, a bloodhound?"

His already stern face turned to stone. He hissed through clenched teeth. "What's it going to take for you to learn some respect for yourself?"

Lori could feel anger rising in her, coloring her face crimson. Still, she stayed silent.

Coach Teller continued to lay into her. "You know what? I'm going to have a little chat with the PTA President. You know her, Julie Haggerty, don't you? If you and the other members of your band don't pull your weight this week leading up to this stupid band battle thing, you're not going to play. How's that sound?"

Meadow interjected, saying, "Coach Teller, Lori didn't mean anything by it, she's just—" but Teller ignored her, never taking his angry, simmering gaze off of Lori.

"You're not done yet. Run another mile, Levi," he said, coldly. Before she could protest, he blew his whistle, gathering the attention of all the other kids around them. "Nice work, y'all! Everybody, but Levi, go inside and enjoy the air conditioning!"

God, I hate Coach Teller so much, Lori thought as she trudged through the hallway leading away from the gymnasium. She was covered in sweat and still wearing her gym clothes. By the time she'd finished the second mile, gym period had finished. The other kids had gone on to their next class, and Teller had locked her out of the locker room, so she couldn't get access to the showers or her day clothes. Now she was late to history *and* was going to be a dirty mess all day.

She looked down at her dorky, off-brand running shoes with their giant rubber soles and swore under her breath, cursing Teller to terrible fates.

She had good reason to hate Teller, but she couldn't understand why he hated *her* so much. For some reason, the man absolutely loathed her and showed it in every way he could. Lecturing her constantly, calling her out in front of classmates, forcing her and no one else to go above and beyond, and threatening to block her from performing in the Battle of the Bands.

Threatening to block her from performing in the Battle of the Bands.

Lori stopped in her tracks in the middle of the hallway. Could it be . . . ? Could the person stalking her be Coach Teller? Would he really go that far? She decided that she had to at least try and find out. And there was no better place to start than in his office.

The coach had a free period at the time, which was why he was able to lock up the gym. He was probably off campus. A lot of teachers went off campus to run errands, get coffee, or, she'd heard, something harder to drink, during their free periods. Lori checked the clock hanging on the wall over the school's trophy case. She had just enough time to sneak down to his office and see what she could find, then make it to her next class like nothing had happened.

She sprinted down the hall to his office, her

exhausted muscles crying out in protest, then slowed as she reached his door. She crept slowly, silently toward it and pressed herself up against the wall next to the door frame.

The door was open, just barely ajar. She had to fight not to laugh out loud. He'd practically left her an invitation.

She reached for the handle and froze when she heard a voice coming from inside the office.

Gruff. Terse. Unmistakably Coach Teller.

She listened for a moment and realized that he was on the phone. It sounded like he was complaining about something. Or someone. *Her*.

". . . her and all her friends, they're trouble," she heard him say. He continued, "Well, yeah, troubled kids. And what do troubled kids do? They cause more trouble. All this grunge business, it's like the hippies when I was a kid."

Lori cringed at being compared to a hippy, but kept listening. Her timing couldn't have been more perfect, and she thought it was pretty likely that he was going to make an admission he couldn't take back.

"But you know what really chaps my rear about this whole Battle of the Bands nonsense?" His voice continued rising in intensity, and Lori could picture the frustrated redness filling his face. It made her smile. "It's that I got a track team full of ace kids."

The track team, Lori thought, her grin fading quickly. Whoever she had chased the night before had been a runner. They were more than just fit; they were a bona fide athlete. Just like Teller.

As kings of the Roosevelt High athletics program,

Coach Teller and Blake weren't exactly strangers either. *Maybe they were working together* . . . The thought turned Lori's blood to ice.

His voice became fainter, as if he was pacing around the room with a cordless phone. She leaned closer to the door. It meant risking being seen, but she absolutely had to hear whatever he said next. The life of her band may depend on it.

"Yeah, right," Teller said to whoever was on the other end of the line. "So my track kids, they're working their tails off. They don't party, they don't let their grades slip, they don't do any *hanky panky*. They're good kids, and they're giving this everything they've got. So, where does that idiot, Juliette Haggerty, put the PTA money? Does she give it to the athletics department so these kids can be rewarded with some new crew socks or something? Nope. She dumps it into this moronic band thing to actually *reward* these kids for their dirtbag behavior. 'Course it benefits her son, doesn't it? He is their guitarist after all. *Oh*, crud! Just saw the time. I gotta go . . . Of course, I'll be there for bird watching on Saturday. Wouldn't miss it . . . Five a.m. Right. I'm gonna find that red-cockaded woodpecker if it's the last thing I do."

Click. Lori listened as he set the phone down in the cradle and began to rummage around his desk.

Her head was swimming. *The PTA money . . . hating the band . . . bird watching?* She didn't have time to unpack it all. Teller was getting his things together for third period and would be out any minute. As Lori turned to hurry away, her sneaker squeaked loudly on the tile floor.

She froze and listened.

Teller had stopped the rummaging in his office. He was clearly doing the same as she was, wise to the fact that someone was spying on him right outside his door and trying to hear who it might be.

Lori considered what to do. She could just run. That made the most sense in the instinctive, animal part of her brain, but she didn't think she could actually get away in time for him not to see her, and she knew he could probably run her down. She could act like she was coming to his office by chance. To do what, though? Apologize? She didn't think she could stomach an act like that. Maybe she could just wait a second, and he'd go back to doing what he was doing.

She was still paralyzed by the options when she heard a hard, intimidating voice behind her.

"Well, Miss Lori Levi. I've got you now."

Chapter 16

Coach Teller advanced on her like a freight train.

"Are you spying on me?" Spittle flew from his lips as he grabbed her by the upper arm, which kept her from running away.

"No, I was just, *um—*" *Ugh. Why lie?* She knew that he would find a way to punish her no matter what. "Maybe. Maybe not. I thought I might catch you *red-handed*."

Teller paused, arched an eyebrow. His grip lessened on her arm, but he didn't let go.

"*Cherry red,*" Lori added.

"What?" His face twisted in genuine confusion.

"Don't play dumb with me, Coach," Lori said, angry now. "Is it just you, or are you working with Blake?"

"Blake? Your ex-boyfriend?"

How did he know they'd dated? Why was he paying attention to things like that? It gave Lori the creeps to think that teachers were paying attention to who students were going out with.

"And the quarterback of the football team. You two know each other quite well, don't you?"

"I know that kid's a soon-to-be full-blown wino.

He's going to drink himself into an early grave and forget any scholarship for that arm of his. 'Sides, if he doesn't get that anger problem under control on the field, he's going to—"

She wrenched her arm from his grasp and stumbled over her own feet as she stepped away from him. "I don't have time for this! Someone is trying to destroy my band, and if it's not you, I'm sure you know who it is!"

Coach Teller stepped toward her and jabbed his finger into her shoulder, hard. His face was stony as he hissed, "I promise you I don't know what you're talking about. Look, I talked to Julie and she agreed with me. You let your grades keep slipping, come into school hungover, or even worse *drunk*? You're finished around here. Not only is there no Battle of the Bands, I'll have you expelled!"

"I'm not going to miss the competition. Period."

"*Oh* yeah? Prove it. Get your act together." His eyes glimmered with cruelty. "But we both know you won't."

It took every bit of self-control she had to not punch him in his big, square, red, stupid face.

"You're a silly, small man, Coach Teller," Lori said.

He smirked. "And your days here are numbered."

Lori turned and marched quickly down the hallway, practically shaking with anger. The guy was a psycho. An absolute psycho.

Your days here are numbered. The words echoed in her mind, sounding more and more like a threat.

Dread and anxiety swirled in Lori's head. She shifted on the hot hood of Seth's car and blinked in the sun as she looked out over the parking lot, waiting for Seth. She needed to talk to him as soon as possible about the deal that Coach Teller had made with Julie, and he was staying late to work. She couldn't recall exactly what he was working on. A science project or something.

Poser. Lori laughed to herself, cutting the tension in her heart for just a moment.

The split second of inner peace died and left her with the question she'd been mulling over ever since her confrontation with Coach Teller: Who was trying to destroy Crying Lilacs? It had to be Blake or Teller, she reasoned. It *had* to be.

Blake was clearly psychotic. She'd learned that fact too late to say no to his first date. Or the second. Too late to say no when he offered her his stupid class ring, and he started checking every day to make sure she was wearing it around her neck on the gold chain he'd put it on. But eventually, she learned it well. Everybody in town thought he was such a nice boy. Clean cut, blond, handsome, from a nice, wealthy family. But he wasn't a boy, he was a young man, and he'd developed into a controlling, possessive jerk who was clearly capable of violence, as he'd shown her that night at the dance.

Then, there was Coach Teller.

He was a molder of men. Boys, really, as far as Lori was concerned. He was infamous for pushing his student athletes to the absolute limit, stopping at nothing to get them to perform. He'd expected the same behavior from his P.E. students and, since starting the band, nobody had pushed back against him more than Lori. If he was willing to investigate her like a drug dog around school, what was stopping him from stalking her off campus as well?

The thought of them working together intrigued Lori, but Coach Teller had such disdain for the quarterback that she was beginning to doubt it.

Maybe Blake should watch his back, too. The thought gave Lori another fleeting moment of pleasure.

"Hey, get offa that car, punk!"

A low, gruff, angry voice cut into Lori's inner monologue, and she snapped back to reality. She jumped in surprise and looked up to find Seth walking toward her with a big goofy smile on his face.

She rolled her eyes and tried to play off the fact that he'd actually scared her. "You creep."

"I'm sorry," he said sincerely. Almost tenderly.

"Whatever, it's fine," she mumbled.

"No, really, I thought that would be funny, but you're on edge. It wasn't cool."

She couldn't hide her feelings from him. They knew each other too well.

"It's fine, for real." She hopped off the hood of his car. "I'm not stalking you, by the way, I just really need to talk to you about—"

"Coach Teller threatening us with our grades and stuff?"

"Okay, now you are freaking me out a little bit . . ."

"*Oh*, it's . . . *uh* . . . I actually talked to my mom already. I used the office phone to call her. Told them it was an emergency, but I just wanted to see what was for dinner. Anyway, she told me he'd called her up about it earlier today. Something about how if we don't keep our grades up or something that he wants her to kick us out of the competition."

"I'm sorry, you called your mom from school to see what was for dinner?" Lori laughed. She didn't mean to hurt his feelings, but she couldn't help it.

He grinned sheepishly and shifted his backpack awkwardly. With his face flushed, he was sort of cute. "It's no big deal, I was just curious."

"Is she gonna have a big ol' Manwich waiting for you when you get home?" she teased.

"You're brutal, Lori," he said, but he was smiling. "She's not gonna do anything, by the way, about the Coach Teller thing. I feel like that's way more important than me being hungry."

That's why I'm here, not to flirt with Seth, Lori reminded herself.

"Right, yeah. What did she say?"

"She said he was a total prick. I mean, she didn't say it like that. But yeah, she said he called her up freaking out, saying we were all wasting our lives with the band, and we were taking drugs, and he was just ranting and raving at her. Totally unhinged. He said he wanted her and the PTA not to let us play, but—" He saw the nervous impatience in Lori's eyes and course corrected. "Sorry, you know all this. Basically, she told him she'd consider it just so he'd get off the phone and leave her alone."

"She's gonna consider it?" Worry rose in Lori's voice.

"She's not gonna do anything about it, I promise."

Lori paced back and forth in tight little lines in front of the car. Five steps here, five steps there. Seth grabbed her by the shoulders, stopping her for a moment, then let go when she looked up into his eyes.

"Trust me, Lori. We're good."

She wanted to believe him. So badly, she wanted to believe him. But that would mean that she'd have to believe his mom. She didn't particularly like the ever well-meaning Julie Haggerty, PTA mother of the year. She didn't think she'd do anything to screw them over, but every adult in her life had taught her otherwise.

She wanted to say that to Seth, but knew it would rub him the wrong way, given how close he was to his mother.

Instead, she just said, "Yeah, all right. We're good."

Gravel crunched under Lori's feet, the only sound in the otherwise humid, quiet night.

As she approached the barn, a calm began to come over her. All the dread was swept away by the knowledge that she'd be able to tuck herself away for a bit with the Jaguar and tape recorder and a notebook and her heart and lose herself in being creative for a bit. When she was writing and playing, nothing else mattered. It was therapy of a sort, even though she hated using that word for it. Therapy was for rich people who could sit around and whine. Whatever it was, though, it made her happy and disconnected her from the world's troubles.

Getting closer, she noticed that the butt-end of an old Gremlin car stuck out from behind the barn. Someone was there.

Worry hit her like a ton of bricks. Goosebumps rose on her arms. Cold sweat broke on the back of her neck. Her eyes darted, wary of who may be out there. Another mask-faced maniac?

Then she remembered: Memphis.

He'd recently inherited the Gremlin from a dead uncle or cousin or someone out there who gave a crap about him. Certainly not his parents. She hadn't gotten used to seeing the car around yet, and it startled her.

For a second, she was annoyed that she wouldn't be alone that night. She really needed a little time to herself. Then she thought about Memphis practicing long into the night, pounding the skins to the metronome, all for the band. Pride and gratitude were all she felt then.

When she got to the barn door, she was hit with the faint smell of pot smoke. She knocked on the open door and called his name softly.

No answer.

She stepped a few feet in, blind in the darkness of the barn, and stumbled over something heavy. As her eyes adjusted, she was able to focus on what had tripped her: a stack of big cardboard boxes with the Ludwig Drums logo emblazoned on their sides.

He'd just gotten a new drum kit with the money from the benefit show, so that explained that, but why hadn't he unpacked it? Furthermore, why hadn't he turned the lights on?

Lori flicked the light switch next to the door. Nothing happened. The electricity had always been a little finicky. *It's just on the fritz again,* Lori told herself.

Battery-powered camping lanterns littered the little barn for just such an occasion. Why wouldn't he turn one on as soon as he came in?

Smoke hovered in the air. *A fire?* Alarmed, Lori grabbed one of the lanterns from a nearby shelf and clicked it to life. Wan yellow light eked out, only illuminating the first few feet in front of her.

Fear rising, she searched for the source of the smoke and found it near one of the Ludwig boxes. A smoldering roach. Smoke trickled up into the air and hovered at eye level.

A smirk played on Lori's lips. It was all making sense.

Memphis had been loading the drums in, just dropping them in the darkened doorway, before turning on the lights and cracking them open. He'd taken a little smoke break, and then he'd heard her coming up the path. *Crunch, crunch, crunch* on the gravel.

He'd taken off into the dark recesses of the barn and was waiting to scare her.

She'd probably walked in right as he took off, dropping his joint, and he hadn't been able to come back for it without her catching him.

Lori shook her head and toed the roach out beneath her sneaker. Red embers breathed their last.

"All right, Memphis!" she called out. "Come on out, dude, I got you." She made her way toward the back of the barn, holding the lantern an arm's length in front of her. The poor light did little to battle against the shadows encroaching on her as she went deeper into the darkness. Rusted farm equipment hung from the walls. The dull metal blades and clamps and sawteeth were so benign in the daytime that she'd barely noticed them. Now, in the night, they threatened to chew her up.

She shook the thought off and pressed on.

"Let's get these boxes unpacked. I'll help you set up the kit. You know, like *always*." She tried to joke, but it felt forced. She reached the back of the barn, where they'd haphazardly stacked or even just thrown their old, broken equipment. Jagged wood and frayed wires reached out at her from the dark.

How had she not found him yet? The barn was a bit cluttered, but not that big. There weren't many places to hide. And it wasn't like Memphis to keep something going like this, long enough to actually scare her. The guy was a sweetheart. He knew when a joke was going too far.

Schinnggg! The sound of metal slicing through air called out through the shadows, and she spun around, heart in her throat, waving the lantern about, trying to locate anything lurking around her.

A small hand scythe stood on its bladed end in the rotting wood of an old workbench, still quivering from the force of falling off its hook.

Lori breathed a sigh of relief and leaned against Meadow's beaten-up four-foot-tall bass amp. Having something to prop herself against kept her on her feet after her legs had turned to Jell-O. At least the piece of junk amp was still good for something.

As she scanned the other side of the barn, she noticed that the door was closed. Had she closed it behind her? Had it creaked shut as she'd walked away and just not heard it? She couldn't be sure . . .

Suddenly, a weight hit her in the back, along her shoulder blades. Something heavy, putting all of its weight against her.

Lori jumped forward and spun around, holding

the lantern up like a life-saving shield, this time with a trembling hand.

The screen of the amp was bowing out. Something was trying to get out of it . . .

"Memphis?" The boy's name came from Lori's lips in a choked whisper.

As if on cue, the amp's screen broke apart and fell outward, letting the thing inside of it come crashing out and fall violently to the cracked, oil-stained concrete floor.

It took a moment for Lori's brain to catch up with what her eyes were telling her.

Memphis lay in a crumpled heap at her feet. Eyes open. Mouth agape. A bass string pulled tight around his purple-hued throat.

"*Oh* no! *Oh no, no, no! Please no!*"

Lori dropped to her knees and set the lantern close to his face so she could see what she was doing. She placed her hand against his open mouth. No air came out. Without a second thought, she pulled the wire away and pressed her lips to his. She blew into his lungs as hard as she could and pumped his chest over and over again, desperately trying to get his breathing going.

A horrible, wheezing rattle emanated from deep within his chest, but no breath came.

Tears streamed down her cheeks as she said the words she hoped someone who loved her would say to her.

"It's going to be okay, Memphis. I got you. I'm not letting go. I'm not letting go of you, okay? You gotta hold onto me!"

She pumped his chest. She breathed for him, but he didn't take it.

The lantern light glinted off his sightless eyes. Her fingers touched flesh growing colder every second. She shook him and held him and begged him to wake up. Deep down, she knew the truth.

Memphis was dead.

Chapter 17

They're supposed to make him look alive, Lori thought, gazing down at Memphis' body in his casket.

He looked so strange with all of the makeup caked on his face. Like a wax figure version of himself. At least they had managed to convincingly cover the horrible mark on his neck from the bass string.

She had the sudden, strange urge to touch him, to caress his cheek or poke him or just shake him and beg for him to wake up, but she couldn't bring herself to reach out. She'd already felt how cold his body had become, and she didn't want to feel it again.

The state room of the funeral home wasn't as full as Lori would have liked—as Memphis deserved—but there was a decent crowd. There were some players from other bands and a relative with a patchy beard who smelled like stale cigarettes and sat in the back, clad in a funeral suit of black jeans and a black denim jacket. The guy who had gifted Memphis the Gremlin, Lori figured. Ms. Wilkins, the guidance counselor, had come. She thought he would have liked that.

Several rows of seats were filled with students. Some she knew, some she didn't. She'd seen all of them dance at their shows, and it felt good to know that they cared enough to come. Seth was there, of course, and so was Julie, mother of the year. They sat in the front row, and Julie had been loudly bawling her eyes out the entire time. Seth acted like he was attached to her hip. Kleenex came out of his suit jacket pockets for her like he was pulling an infinite rainbow scarf out of a clown's mouth. While Julie wouldn't stop caterwauling, Seth, for his part, vacillated between looking heartbroken, nauseous, and frightened.

He was so sensitive. Sometimes Lori liked that about him, but other times, like now, she wished that he'd be a little stronger. She needed someone to lean on, even if she didn't want to show it.

Meadow shuffled up next to Lori at the coffin, sniffling. Mascara streaked down her cheeks. She hadn't been able to quit crying since Lori had picked her up to attend the funeral.

Lori put her arm around her friend and held her tight to her side.

Meadow reached out as if to touch Memphis, but stopped. They stood there together for what felt like an eternity to Lori, but may have only been a second.

Finally, Lori said, "I couldn't touch him either."

Meadow dug around in her purse for a moment until she found what she was looking for. The Kiss Zippo lighter. She flicked it open and thumbed the flint, and the two young women watched the flame dance until Meadow snapped it shut.

She took a deep breath, then reached down and slid the Zippo in between Memphis' folded hands, lingering just long enough to feel his touch one last time.

That's strength, Lori thought, admiring her friend.

"They put him in a suit," Meadow murmured, more to herself than Lori. "He hated suits. And his hair is all combed and dorky. They made him look like an accountant."

"Come on, let's get some fresh air," Lori said.

She took Meadow by the hand and led her up the narrow aisle between the chairs, past the staring, stricken faces, and outside into the sun-drenched day.

The duo sat down on the stairs leading to the front door of the funeral home. On cue, without a word, they both removed packs of cigarettes and placed one each between their lips. Lori lit hers with a Bic and took a deep drag.

"I . . . I don't have a lighter," Meadow said.

Lori laughed, and then Meadow laughed, and then they both wished so desperately that their friend could be there to understand that moment, to get the humor in the way that he would have, and so many others couldn't.

When the laughter died down, Lori lit Meadow's smoke for her.

"How are you holding up?" Meadow asked. "I can't imagine finding him like you did. I-I-I'm so sorry you had to see that, Lori."

"Well, at least he wasn't in a suit then," Lori said.

A little more dark humor to get them through. Meadow snickered ruefully.

"No, but seriously, are you okay?"

"I-I don't know," Lori said. The truth was, she

didn't want to talk about it. She couldn't think about it. The terror. The pain. It was too much.

She said, "The thing that breaks my heart is . . . this funeral, I mean, it's great, people came, people cared, but . . . it's a reflection of the life he wanted to leave behind. He was destined to live this long, cool life, where hundreds of fans and tons of like, hot ex-wives came to his funeral, and he was buried in this giant rich guy mausoleum. Imagine a dozen beautiful women behind black veils, all crying in the back of his funeral."

Meadow laughed again.

"He wasn't destined to die here," Lori said.

Meadow took a long drag of her cigarette and then said, "Then why's he in that box?"

Lori didn't know how to answer that.

They heard someone clear their throat behind them and turned to find Seth standing there, leaning against the closed doors to the funeral home.

"I don't want to intrude, I can go back inside," he said gently.

"Yeah, right. Sit down, weirdo." Meadow slapped the space of cement between them.

Seth took the seat. Meadow held out a cigarette for him. Gingerly, he slid it from the pack and placed it awkwardly between his lips. When he saw the look of surprise on Lori's face, he gave her a sad grin and said, "Today's the day for it."

Lori flicked the Bic to life and lit his cigarette for him. He inhaled and coughed a little.

"I'm sorry for my mom. She can really get emotional. Like, she has trouble not making a scene sometimes."

"It's okay. It's actually kind of sweet," Lori said, and meant it.

"Can I ask you guys something?"

"Sure," Meadow said.

"Why do—*er*, did—why *did* we call him Memphis? I know it wasn't his real name, and Lori, I know you wanted him to tell me, so I get it if you don't want to share but I just had to ask. Is it something crazy? Like Indiana Jones getting named after the dog or something?"

Lori looked at Meadow and raised her eyebrows. *You can tell him if you want.* Meadow nodded solemnly.

"Yeah, of course. Y-You can know. It's actually because, well . . . his dad was from there, from Memphis, Tennessee. And when his mom was pregnant with him, his dad would tell her all about how great it is there and how after their son was born, he was going to move them back there and get a good job and they'd have this like, awesome life, all together as a family." Meadow took a long drag on her cigarette, like she was charging up her battery so that she could finish the story. "So then, one day, his mom, like, goes into labor, right? Like, the baby is coming, and it's coming *fast*."

Lori and Seth laughed at that, the image of baby Memphis flying out of his mother, ready for the world.

"But the dad, he's not there. He was out drinking with his friends, right? There's no time to call and try to find him or whatever, so she has to drive herself to the hospital. When she gets there, she's going into labor hardcore, and she's like, 'Call this bar and this bar, until you get my husband. Tell him the baby's coming.' They weren't really married, not yet, but you get it. So they're calling around, she's just doing her thing, being a badass mom.

"She gives birth to her son without the dad being there. All on her own. Then they ask her what to name him, for the birth certificate, and she hadn't decided on a name yet, but the first thing that pops into her head is Memphis. The city of dreams, right? So she names him that. It actually is on his birth certificate. It's his legal name."

"Wow, that's incredible that she did that all on her own," Seth said.

"Yeah, it is," Meadow replied, but she didn't sound enthusiastic. "But the dad . . . he never comes. They call every bar in town. Then every adult club. Then every hospital. They never found him."

"Wait, so they never found him? Did he die?" Seth asked, incredulous.

"No, dummy. He bailed. Memphis' mom thinks that the bartender at the first bar, where she thought he was, pretended he wasn't there. Secretly, he told him the baby was coming. He got in his car and just like, took off. They never saw him again."

"I can't believe someone could do that to their own kid."

"Happens all the time," Meadow said. "His name was always this promise of something great that would never happen. He used to say in private, when it was just him and me, that he was cursed by that name. I never believed him. Now I do."

A sad, but comfortable quiet settled in between the three of them as they gazed out at the sunny day, the stillness of it all, the humming of bugs, and the distant rumble of cars as life went on all around them.

Movement caught Lori's eye behind a tree lining the edge of the funeral home's small parking lot. A blue blur poking out from behind a big, thick oak. It was a familiar shade of blue. The same as Roosevelt High's colors. The same that would be found on the school's letterman jackets.

"No way. Not today. It can't be him," Lori said.

"*Huh?*" Meadow said, her voice spacey and removed, like she'd barely been listening.

Lori stubbed out her cigarette and marched toward the tree. As she got closer, she heard low talking and laughing. She stormed around the wide trunk to find Blake and one of his football buddies, Evan or whatever, a linebacker or something, she thought, leaning against the tree. Smirks plastered across their faces. A near-empty twelve-pack of Milwaukee's Best sat in the overgrown grass at their feet.

"What are you doing here?" Lori asked through gritted teeth.

"*Ooooh!*" Evan or whatever mimicked a sitcom audience reaction, like '*Somebody's in trouble!*'

"Shut up," she hissed to the linebacker or something, then narrowed her eyes at Blake. "I'll ask again, dude, what do you think you're doing here?"

"Relax, babe. School said if we wanted to come, they'd let us out early. We figured we'd ditch math and come on down. Catch the freak show," Blake said with a sloppy grin.

Evan let out a dumb, keening laugh and threw out his palm. Blake slapped it.

"*Freak show?* How dare you?" Lori seethed. "I

know exactly why you're here. You're here to torture us. Me and the rest of the band. To mock us, to rub our faces in this tragedy because—"

Blake waved his hand in the air as if he were swatting lazily at a fly, dismissing her and her anger. "I'm just busting your chops, Lori. You used to be so cool. Here . . ." He reached down, rummaged in the beer box, and came back with a sweaty can of Milwaukee's. He held it out for her. "Take a breather and crack a brewski with us."

Lori violently slapped the can from his hand. It sailed through the air and landed on the pavement of the nearby parking lot. The can split open, spraying beer and suds, and the force of the carbonation sent it skittering over the cracked asphalt.

"What a waste," Evan muttered.

Lori ignored him. She kept her sights on Blake, boring into him with a glare.

She said, "I know you had something to do with this. I know it. And as soon as we bury Memphis, I mean the *second* that he's put into the ground, I'm going to the police, and I'm turning you in."

Blake's faux jovial expression immediately slid from his face and was replaced by a look of hate and rage, a darkness like she'd never seen from him before.

"I didn't have anything to do with his murder, and if you say a thing to the police, they're gonna laugh you outta the station. And you know what? It doesn't really even matter who did it, probably some other drugged-out grunge freak you guys know. But it doesn't matter, because in the end, this stupid thing you're doing, chasing your dumb dreams and this scummy lifestyle, it's gonna kill all of you."

"Is that some kind of *threat*?" Lori asked.

"Call it whatever you want. You're all gonna die."

Chapter 18

Four cigarette butts smouldered at Lori's feet. She'd been standing in front of the police station for—she checked her watch—twenty-three minutes. If she took any more time, they'd come out and arrest her for loitering.

She couldn't believe she was about to walk into a police station. But at this point, what other options were there?

She took a deep breath and went up the wide stone steps leading to the double doors. They seemed massive, impossibly heavy. Everything weighed so heavily on her these days.

A skinny little beanpole of a policeman sat behind a desk. He blinked at her through a pair of Coke-bottle glasses and licked the corners of his lips, where white scum had collected. So much for a welcoming committee. She squared her shoulders and laid her hands palm down on the counter, projecting an air of what she hoped was authority.

"I need to speak to a, *uh*." An agent? No, that wasn't right. "A detective," she said, finally.

He stared at her. Owlish eyes probed through the thick glasses.

"It's about the... the murder of Memphis. Memphis O'Brien," she said with a shudder.

A look of vague recognition passed over the man's thin, pale face.

Five minutes later, she was sitting at a detective's desk. Clutter was everywhere. Stacks of files and paperwork stood like plateaus in the desert. The detective sat back in her rolling chair and eyed Lori coolly. She was broad-shouldered and a bit of a belly fought against the buttons of her Hawaiian shirt.

The sound of heavy panting startled Lori, and she turned to her left to find an enormous German Shepherd sitting only a couple of feet away from her. He wore a collar but wasn't leashed to anything. He stared at her as if he could read the depths of her soul. What was he doing there?

A drug dog, Lori realized. *They've let him loose on me. I come to them for help, and they look for a way to arrest me.*

The detective shifted heavily in her seat. A scowl creased her freckled face. Tan, lightly weathered skin was pulled back tight by the ponytail tied atop her head.

"Your name?" The detective spoke with a drawl to rival Coach Teller's.

"Lori." Lori searched the woman's broad chest for a nametag but found only crossed, muscular arms and hula girls on her shirt. Plain clothes, no uniform. "What's your name, Offi—"

"*Detective*. My name is Detective Threatt."

"*Threatt*?"

"Lucky coincidence for me, *eh*?" Detective Threatt gave a terse laugh and casually picked a bit of lint off her khaki slacks. "You are the one who found the body, correct?"

Lori knew that cops would take whatever you said and twist it around. They wanted to put people like Lori—trailer park people from the wrong side of town, people who nobody would miss, heck, people who decent society would like to see gone—in prison. They wanted clean cases. That meant eliciting confessions, pressuring people to turn on friends and family.

"The *body*? You mean Memphis? My friend?"

"Yes. Memphis. Your friend. Do you mind if I ask you some questions?"

Lori leaned across the desk, invading the woman's space. "Actually, I have a question for you. Like, when are you gonna catch whoever did this? Also, if you need help, I think I can give it to you. How about that? That was two questions, I guess."

A grin played upon Detective Threatt's lips and then quickly vanished.

"You've got guts, Lori. You ask me a question, and I'll ask you a question, how's that?"

"I don't have a question. I need to tell you that I know who did it."

"*Oh*, yeah? Who's that?"

"Blake Cutler," she said firmly. Then her mind began to spin with the other possibilities, and her confidence faltered. Quickly, she added, "Or, or maybe and, I'm not quite sure yet, Coach Teller. He claims they aren't working together, but—"

"Blake Cutler? The quarterback for Roosevelt High and Coach Teller murdered your buddy Memphis?"

Lori sighed deeply. She should have known that Blake's reputation would have preceded him. One more hurdle for her to jump. "I know how it sounds, but—"

The detective dropped her elbows onto the desk and leaned forward, nearly knocking over a file labeled 'Blockbuster Robbery — Mugshots.' She ignored it and said, "Sure, you do. Let's go on this journey for a moment. Pretend I believe you. Why would they murder him?"

"To destroy my band and stop us from winning the Battle of the Bands."

As soon as Lori said it, she realized how ridiculous it sounded. That didn't make it any less true, though.

Detective Threatt began to laugh. Long, peeling laughs that shook her whole body. Tears welled in her eyes. She caught her breath and wiped her eyes with the palms of her hands. Finally, she asked, "They murdered a high school kid because they don't like your band?"

Lori's face flushed with rage and embarrassment. She rose from her seat, and the dog next to her stood up and growled. Lori paused, looking from the dog to the detective. She was running hot. She had to force herself not to lash out at the cop. To remain calm. Lori sat back down.

In the best measured, easy tone she could manage, she said, "Yes. Again, I know that sounds crazy or dumb or whatever to you, but it's true."

"I have a question for you, Lori. This one is actually serious. Did Memphis wrestle with feelings of depression? Anxiety and inadequacy? He didn't have much family support, did he? Bit of an outcast too, right? A loner?"

Lori suddenly realized what the detective was getting at.

"He did *not* kill himself! He wasn't even hanging or—Whatever, it doesn't matter. He would *never*. We loved him. We were his family."

"Is what I just asked you true or not?" Detective Threatt pushed.

"Well, *um* . . ."

"I'm gonna let you think about that for a minute while I go get us some sodas. You can sit here with K-9 Ralphie. He's our best." She winked at Lori and turned to the beast beside her, who was still standing at alert. "Aren't you, Ralphie? Yes, you're the best we've got!" The dog wagged its tail. "All right, I'll be back in a few. Don't go anywhere." She then turned and walked away.

Lori eyed the dog. Detective Threatt said he was a professional, so maybe he was friendly to people who weren't holding any contraband. Lori quickly patted her pockets to make sure she didn't have anything on her. No, she was safe.

Maybe she could make friends with him. Maybe if they could bond, the detective would see that she was all right. On the level, as they say.

"Cops say that, right? On the level?" she asked the dog.

The German Shepherd growled. The sound came from deep in its chest, low and rumbling. Threatening.

"*Oh* come on, we can be friends," Lori said, but her tone said she wasn't so sure about it either.

The dog stood and took an aggressive step toward her, its teeth bared.

"Good *uh*, p-puppy," Lori stammered. "You're a police dog, you're a good boy."

Tentatively, she reached out a shaking hand to pet him . . .

Before she could make contact, the dog lunged at her, teeth glinting, jaws snapping around her hand.

Chapter 19

A fist gripped the collar of the snarling beast and yanked it back. The dog's jaws clamped shut centimeters away from Lori's fingers.

She gasped and instinctively checked her hand, amazed that she was still whole.

Lori looked up from the growling dog to the man holding it back. The face was familiar, but she was still so in shock from the dog lunging at her that she couldn't place who he was ... Then it hit her like a brick.

It was the sweaty yuppie from the show. The one who had given her such a strange, unsettling feeling. The one who had grabbed her arm. The polo shirt and slacks were gone. Now he was wearing a police officer's uniform.

Suddenly, she wished she were dealing with the dog instead.

He waved over another officer who hurried, took the German Shepherd by the collar, and trotted it away. Then he squatted down onto the balls of his feet so that he was at her level. The sweat was gone, his hair was in place. Still, he had an intensity in his gaze that gave her an odd, cold feeling.

"Sorry, ma'am, for K-9 Ralphie, he's a rookie. Not through training yet. Shouldn't have been out here in the bullpen without a muzzle. That's just—" He did a double take, then leaned in closer until he was just inches from her face. "I know you," he said softly, almost in a whisper.

"I . . . I know you, too," she said back.

"I was at your show, the one at the bowling alley. The square old man," he said, and giggled, high and tittering.

"Yeah. I remember." Lori shifted uncomfortably in her chair. She wished like hell that the dog would come back. It could even bite her. At least then she could get a swift exit ride out of there in an ambulance.

"I gave you guys a lot of money that night. I guess it's obvious, but I'm a big fan. Bet you didn't think cops liked rock n' roll, *huh?* Especially a band like yours. You guys rock pretty hard." When she didn't respond, he said, "Why are you here? Maybe I can help you."

"I'm here to report the person that I know, *er*, well, think I know killed my bandmate."

"Memphis." He shook his head. "I heard about that. Tragic. Just tragic, Lori. I'm surprised you didn't fly away after seeing something like that."

Then he touched her leg, his long, bony fingers dancing lightly along the top of her thigh like this weird spider she'd once seen walk on water in a nature documentary, before snatching his hand away and making it flit through the air, mimicking the motion of a bird.

"Just fly away from this town . . ." He said it wistfully, as if suddenly lost in a fantasy.

This guy is a cop? Lori thought. *He's acting like a total whack job.*

She scooted back in her chair, trying in vain to put some distance between them. Scanning his chest for a nametag, she found nothing. Strange. A cop with no name. She didn't know what to say. She was afraid of offending him. Could he arrest her for offending him?

"That detective lady, what's-her-name, *uh*, Threatt, I'm talking to her. She's coming back soon, she said, so . . ."

So get out of my face, weirdo.

Instead of taking the hint, the cop leaned in until he was just inches from her face. He whispered, "She won't be back for a long time."

"What do you mean?" Lori asked, pulling away from him, trying not to betray the disgust she was feeling. "Why not?"

"Same reason she let you sit with that naughty drug dog," he said. "She's letting you sweat it out. She wants to see if you have something to confess."

"Something to confess? But I didn't do anything."

His gaze was almost hypnotic then. Not appealing in any way, but it still pulled her in, forced her eyes to his own. A hideous car wreck she couldn't look away from, even if it was about to explode and swallow her in its flames.

Quietly, he said, "The bad part about being a cop—the part nobody wants to talk about—is that sometimes that doesn't matter."

Suddenly, it felt like everyone in the precinct was

watching her. Studying her. Accusing her. Forcing herself to avert his gaze, Lori looked around the room, hoping to catch them in the act, but they were all making phone calls or sending faxes or doing paperwork or just standing around.

Still, somehow, she could feel their eyes on her. Hot, acidic nausea rose inside her.

"I'd like to go home now," she murmured, her tongue suddenly thick and dry in her mouth, a slug doused with salt. "Can—Or, *uh*, may I go home now?"

"*Oh*, Lori, of course you can. You're not in any trouble. Not yet."

His face broke into a wide grin. Something about his teeth unsettled her. Not that they were crowded or dirty or broken. The opposite. They were perfect. All straight and pristinely white. They made him seem . . . *unreal*. Like a doll, a mannequin man.

"When you leave, please remember, no matter where you go, you're safe. I've got my eye on you."

"I knew they wouldn't be any help," Meadow said. "They don't care. Not about us, anyway. Maybe the kids up in Candle Hill."

Meadow side-eyed Seth, but he ignored her in favor of the double cheeseburger steaming in front of him.

Lori, Meadow, and Seth sat in the back booth of Andy's Grill, a greasy spoon spot that had been in town for a million years, near as any of them could tell. When Lori had called them all together for a band meeting, she'd first planned to have them meet up at the barn. Then she considered having to step foot inside of it for the first time since finding Memphis' body, and her skin broke out in gooseflesh, and she couldn't stop sweating.

Instead, she'd opted for Andy's. She could feel their relief at not having to go back to the scene of the gruesome crime when she told them over the phone.

The barn, once the safest place on earth, was just one more thing that had been taken from them. Now her band sat in the back corner booth, listening to Lori tell them about her horrible trip to the police station while she fought back the sick feeling that rose in her gut from the reek of grease that hung in the air around them.

"We have to take care of ourselves now," Lori said.

Meadow didn't look up from the cheese fries she'd been picking at. In the whole time they'd been sitting there, she'd had maybe three fries. Lori hadn't been able to even consider eating. She sipped on her Diet Pepsi.

There was a long moment of silence, punctuated only by the clatter of pans and the muffled yells of cooks back in the kitchen.

Finally, Lori said, "We need to keep rehearsing for the Battle."

In a weak voice, Lori could barely hear, Meadow asked, "Where will we get a drummer?"

Lori shot Seth a look that said, *Now's the time. Fess up.* He took a deep breath, pushed his half-eaten cheeseburger away.

"I . . . I have a drum kit. I have a lot of instruments, actually. A studio setup. I can play drums. Not, you know, as well as Memphis, obviously. He was the best. But I can fill in if I have to."

Meadow dropped the fry she'd been idly holding. Surprise and anger flared in her eyes. "You had all this stuff the whole time? Why didn't you tell us? We played that fundraising show and everything for no reason!"

"Because I knew that this is how you'd look at me. Like I was a rich, spoiled little jerk."

That deflated Meadow's anger a bit. "Can't argue with that," she mumbled, and turned back to her fries.

"Look, Mead, cards on the table, I knew about it as well," Lori said. "I agreed with Seth that he shouldn't tell because it makes you guys look at him a certain way and, well, even I kinda looked at him that way." She turned to Seth. "Sorry about that. But Mead, Seth is a great player, you know that. We need him. We need each other. See, he and I—we—agreed that we'd share that info if and when we really needed it. We really, really need it now. We can't give up. We need to stick together. Not just for the win, for the record deal, for all of that, but for Memphis. He can't have died for no reason. He just . . . we can't let that happen."

Tears welled in Lori's eyes, and she realized she needed to end her little inspirational speech. Seth and Meadow sat in silence. Neither looked up from the table. She hadn't expected them to erupt into cheers, but her passionate plea wasn't having the effect she'd hoped.

Finally, Seth broke the quiet. "Is this really a good idea? I mean . . . somebody hates this band so much that they *murdered* Memphis. I . . . I can't be the only one terrified by that. Is this really worth it?"

"Maybe not to you, rich boy," Meadow said, but the tone in her voice sounded less convinced, like she really just wanted to throw a barb at Seth.

For his part, Seth ignored Meadow's blow. Instead, he locked eyes with Lori for the first time during their entire conversation. His gaze asked her, pleadingly, *Is it really worth it?*

She couldn't answer the question. She was torn. Destroyed. Crying Lilacs was her band, so it was her creativity, *and* it was her responsibility. She didn't want more people to get hurt, but she didn't want to give up and let the person stalking them, hurting them, killing them, to win.

Did she really want to do this for Memphis, for her other bandmates? Or was this her own stupid pride? She believed it was the former, but deep, deep down, she wondered if it was just her own selfish need to prove to everyone that she was somebody.

The question ate her alive.

"You're right, Seth. The path forward is dangerous. It's wrong of me to pressure you guys to take that risk. We'll take a vote. If I'm outvoted, we're not moving forward. And if you really don't want to continue, I won't fight you dropping out."

"So, what? We just, like, raise our hands or something?" Meadow asked.

"Sure. That works. Who thinks we should move forward? Raise your hand."

Lori's hand shot up immediately.

Meadow sighed. Chewed on her bottom lip. Fiddled with a cold, limp french fry in her tray. Then, slowly, her hand rose to half-height. Barely a yes, but Lori would take it.

The two of them turned to Seth. He squirmed in his seat. His face flushed pink.

"Yeah, okay." He threw his hand up for a second and then let it drop.

Lori broke out in a huge grin. "We're gonna win this! You'll see. We can't let whoever this is destroy us. We're doing the right thing. Thank you guys."

Meadow nodded. She wasn't smiling, but Lori knew her friend well enough to know that she was committed. Meadow didn't do anything that she didn't want to do.

Seth looked just as worried as he had before the vote.

"How are we going to protect ourselves?" he asked.

"I was thinking about that," Lori said, trying to muster all the confidence she could. It was time to lead. Time to keep her friends safe. As safe as she could, at least. "We're instituting a buddy system. First, we stick together as much as possible, leading up to the Battle of the Bands. With all three of us together, we're way harder to mess with. We'll call each other each morning when we wake up and at night before we go to bed. If we have to separate during the day, we'll check in at the two-hour mark. We need to exchange phone numbers for all of our usual hangouts. Our houses, friends, and family, anywhere you might regularly be."

"What's the number for the country club?" Meadow asked Seth. Her tone now was a bit softer. Almost warm, but not quite.

Seth let out a hard, terse laugh in reply.

"Sound good?" Lori asked the two of them.

"Yeah, that works for me," Meadow said.

Seth nodded. Then, in a small voice, he murmured, "I still have a really bad feeling about this."

Chapter 20

The tape recorder whirred on Lori's bedside table. She plucked a single minor note on the Jaguar and let it sing out through the practice amp at her feet. Another piece of equipment, borrowed from Seth. Sitting on her bed, she cradled the guitar lovingly in her lap and tapped her foot on the floor.

She plucked another note, then another, letting each of them drone out, full of reverb. Full of sadness and pain. She coaxed the feelings from the strings, letting it all out.

Lori didn't know where the song was taking her, but she knew that, in the end, it would be for Memphis.

She jumped as a gunshot rang out. Then the clomping of... horse hooves? It was the TV, echoing through her cheap, pressboard door.

"What are you watching in there?" Lori hollered at her mother.

"Watching my stories!" Amber shouted back. Her words were slurred, like she was already on the edge of passing out. "It's that *Brisco County Jr.* on. I love him."

Lori rolled her eyes. She took a deep breath and

tried to focus on the song, but she'd lost it. Wherever she was headed had evaporated. The creative path was gone, obstructed by her own scattered mind. Well, that and *Brisco County Jr.*

A metallic rattling sound called out from the living room. At first, she thought it was part of the TV show, then realized it was very real. The sound of a doorknob.

Someone was trying to get into their trailer.

"Lori, there's someone knocking at the door! I told your friends not to be so late!" her mom shouted.

Lori launched herself from the bed. The Jaguar landed on the ground with a dull thud. *Sorry, baby*, she thought, but she didn't bother to pick it up. She flung her bedroom door open and sprinted down the dim wood-paneled hallway, heading toward the living room.

"They're not knocking mom, they're trying to break in!"

"Whatever," Amber muttered, her head lolling to the side.

Lori raced through the living room and leaped over her mother's splayed legs, knocking over a wine bottle in the process. She reached the door just as whoever was on the outside threw their body against the door. She gripped the rattling knob and pounded her fist against the door.

"Who's there?" she demanded.

No answer came. Her mother began to mumble something, and Lori put a finger to her lips, shushing her. She pressed her ear to the door and listened.

Scrüittttcchhhh.

A long scraping sound cried out from the other

side of the door, like someone running a gardening claw against the wood. Lori stepped back in horror, eyes wide, fist pressed against her open mouth.

"*Looorrriiiii... Looorrriiiii...*" a lilting, high-pitched voice came from beyond the door.

Heart pounding, Lori grabbed a nearby wooden chair, a remnant from the days when they had a dining room set, and jammed it up under the doorknob. She turned to her mother to tell her to get inside her room and barricade the door, but the woman was passed out cold, snoring on the sofa.

She hurried to the couch. She dropped to her knees and began trying to wake Amber.

Outside, the voice continued to call her name in that sinister, sing-song tone.

"*Looorrriiiii... Looorrriiiii...*"

Lori tried everything to jolt her mother awake, shaking her by the shoulders, lightly slapping her face. The drunk woman's eyes fluttered. A groan of protest escaped her lips, sounding like an angry raspberry, and she swatted at her daughter.

Scrüüttttcchhhh went the claw against the door.

"Leave us alone!" Lori cried out to the stranger.

Her voice cut through the small trailer like a burst of thunder and left silence in its wake. No singing. No scratching.

Maybe they left, Lori thought for a moment, which was immediately followed by, *Yeah, right.*

Still, the silence couldn't be any worse than the horrible sounds the stranger was making, could it? Lori rose and leaned awkwardly over her sleeping mom. She peeked through the broken, yellowed plastic blinds, trying to get at the proper angle to see the door. It was tough to make out, but she could just barely see the sagging wooden steps leading up to the trailer. There was no one there.

The blinds clacked shut as she leaned away from the window. Lori breathed a sigh of relief.

Then, suddenly, the knob began to rattle again, so violently that the entire door shook in its frame.

Lori shrieked and took off. She didn't want to leave her mother behind, but she couldn't deadlift her and carry her to safety. Her only hope was to get to the phone in time to call the police. The closest phone hung on the wall right next to the front door. Not an option. She raced down the hall, heart pounding in her throat, and slammed her bedroom door shut behind her.

Lori locked the door, but knew the flimsy deterrent wouldn't hold back an intruder for long. She launched herself across her bed and grabbed the phone from its cradle on her bedside table.

With a trembling finger, Lori typed in 9 . . . 1 . . . then, a tapping sound came from her closed window. A slow, quiet, tinkling sound. Her finger froze over the final number. The static sound of the void beyond fell away from her ear as the phone slipped from her hand and tumbled to the floor.

She crawled on her hands and knees across the bed to the window over her headboard. Heavy black curtains hung over the window, keeping the threat beyond hidden. The tapping continued, a thin, hollow, dead sound that filled her with dread.

Slowly, she pulled the curtain back and looked into the darkness.

A pale white face swam in the murky night beyond,

the features obscured by shadows in the dull moonlight.

For an instant, she thought she was looking at a white version of the featureless black mask worn by her stalker. A crazy idea flashed in her mind. Was this the light to the dark? Some kind of positive inverse of the evil force that had been working against her? An angel sent to warn her?

A laugh rang out from the formless face, and she knew exactly who it was.

Blake.

He stepped closer to the window, and the light from her bedroom fully illuminated him. Hateful eyes glinted at her. Bloodless lips were drawn tight in a mirthless smirk. He pressed his forehead against the glass. His cruel gaze cut into her. "I heard you've been gossipping about me . . ." he said.

"What . . . what are you talking about?" She'd never seen him quite like this before. He'd been awful in the past, but this time, he looked . . . *evil.*

"A little birdie told me you went to the police . . ."

She wondered who could have told him. The cop with no name? Was it possible they knew each other somehow?

"Who told you?"

"So it is true." The icy grin on his face fell away. "You know, it really hurts me that you think I would do something to harm you. I'm here to protect you, Lori, always. Why don't you let me in? We can talk."

"You want me to invite you in . . . like a vampire."

"That's funny. You're funny, Lori. Let me in, and we'll talk. I'll stay up all night protecting you against whoever is really doing this. Let me be your knight,

Lori. You'll see how much you need me. We can get back to what works. You and me. The band, Lori . . . it's brought you nothing but trouble. You see that now, right? Leave all that behind and let me help you."

Lori backed away across the bed, fumbling behind her for the phone. Finally, she found it, just as she nearly fell off the bed. She held it up like a weapon before her.

"Leave, Blake. Now. Or I'll call the cops again. Attempted breaking and entering. They might love you now, but they won't after that."

His eyes narrowed like a snake. His thick, pink tongue ran over his lips. He backed away into the darkness and vanished.

Lori hurried to the window and pulled the curtains tight. Shuddering, she grabbed a pillow and pulled it to herself, burying her face into it. She wanted to scream. She wanted to cry. But she wouldn't give him the satisfaction.

She knew he was still out there in the dark, watching. Waiting.

Chapter 21

Lori woke with a start, panic gripping her. Her nightmare was drifting off into nothing, leaving her with no memory of the actual dream, only the lingering feeling of absolute horror from whatever had come to her in her sleep.

Her eyes darted around the room as she worked through the haze of waking to confirm that she was in her own space, in her bed, alone.

The sheets were soaked with flop sweat. Errant locks of hair clung to her clammy forehead. But she was safe—as safe as she could be, anyway, behind the locked door and windows of her room. No Blake. No masked attacker. She breathed a sigh of relief.

The feeling was short-lived once she looked at her clock. Nine thirty in the morning. Well past her intended wakeup. It was a Saturday, so school didn't matter. Her concern was Meadow and Seth. She was supposed to have been in contact with them by nine o'clock every morning, if not before.

Lori snatched the phone off the cradle and punched in the number to Seth's private bedroom line. He answered after two rings, his voice sounding distant and strained on the other end.

"Hello? Who is this?"

"It's Lori, dude. Who do you think?"

"*Oh*, yeah, of course. Sorry. Are you okay?"

"Yeah, I'm fine. Are you? You sound weird."

"*Huh?* I sound . . . *Uh* . . ." He let out a long yawn. "I'm just tired. I was up all night. I guess . . ." She heard him fumbling with an alarm clock. "*Oh* man, I must have just fallen asleep."

"Why couldn't you sleep?" she asked, concerned that Blake may have gone after him as well.

"Nothing in particular, I'm just super worried, you know? About Meadow. About you."

"I'm worried about you, too. Speaking of Meadow, I should call her to check in. Let's meet up at Andy's in an hour, though, okay? We'll get you some coffee."

Seth's laughter traveled through the phone, and Lori blushed.

"Sounds good. I'll see you both there."

Lori said goodbye and pressed down on the phone's receiver, then released the button. She dialed Meadow's number and clamped it between her ear and shoulder.

The phone rang. And rang. And rang some more. Finally, it went to the answering machine. Meadow's mother's chipper voice intoned that no one was home right now, but to call back later and—

Lori hung up the phone, then dialed once more. Again, nothing but endless ringing.

Something was wrong; she could feel it deep in her bones.

Meadow was in trouble.

***

Lori wrestled the steering wheel of the truck into submission as she pulled onto the street leading to Meadow's house. It was a modest neighborhood. Split-level ranch houses with small, but usually tidy lawns. The people here had to maintain their own property, not by hiring landscapers, and they did it with pride.

Meadow's house was tucked into the back of the subdivision, at the end of a cul-de-sac. Lori thought of the afternoons the two of them had spent playing out there. Roller blading, drawing with chalk, just talking away for hours. She smiled at the memories and prayed that she would arrive to find Meadow safe and sitting in the middle of the quiet cul-de-sac, scrawling doodles of big flowers and googly-eyed monsters on the asphalt, like she was a little kid again.

As she pulled up to Meadow's house, her dream was dashed.

The place was a hive of police activity. Cops scurried about the lawn. They popped in and out of the house with nervous energy. They examined the flower beds and walkways of the yard, looking for who-knew-what. They ran yellow caution tape around the perimeter of the property, blocking it off from public access while drawing all the attention they could from neighbors.

The truck hadn't even come to a stop before Lori started to open her door. Balding tires kicked up over the curb, and she slammed on the brakes. Forgetting to pull on the parking brake, Lori yanked the keys free and leapt from the car. Some of the cops nearest the street stared slack-jawed at the words spray-painted all over it. She sprinted under the caution tape, ignoring the cop who yelled useless warnings at her, and looked around for Meadow's mother. She knew instinctively that Meadow herself would not be there.

"Mrs. Varnelle? Mrs. Varnelle?!" Lori cried out into the chaos swirling around her.

Lori wondered if the nameless officer with the terrible grin was there. She decided to keep a lower profile and stopped shouting.

Mrs. Varnelle, Meadow's mother, stepped from the house, looking around for the source of the yelling with anxious, red-rimmed eyes. When she found Lori, a small, sad smile pulled at her lips. She stepped across the yard in bare feet and embraced her daughter's friend.

At first, Lori was taken aback by how tightly Mrs. Varnelle clung to her, and she stiffened. But then she gave in to the hug and let herself be of comfort to the woman. Finally, after Lori thought she might pass out from having the breath squeezed out of her, Mrs. Varnelle stepped back, and Lori was able to get a good look at her.

She was disheveled, wearing stained sweatpants and a t-shirt with Bart Simpson on it and a speech bubble that read, "Don't have a cow, man!" Her dirty blonde hair was up in a messy bun, and she was without makeup. Lori could see the age and stress that creased her face. Much like her daughter, Mrs. Varnelle had always seemed so happy-go-lucky, but now, for the first time, Lori simply thought she looked . . . *old*. She was ashamed of having the thought.

"Thank you for coming over," Mrs. Varnelle said. "Who told you what happened? Has the news spread that fast?"

"No, no, I-I had a deal with Meadow where we..." She hesitated. How much did Mrs. Varnelle really know about what had been happening with Crying Lilacs? Her own mother barely knew a thing, and she aimed to keep it that way. What was she supposed to say anyway? *We're being stalked by a murderer, so we have to keep constant tabs on each other, or we'll die. Sure, Mrs. Varnelle, I'd love some lemonade!* No, best to keep it all to herself, at least until she figured out what was going on. "I tried to call the house, and nobody answered, so I got worried. I came over to check on Meadow and..." Lori gestured helplessly around at the cops.

"You're such a good friend," Mrs. Varnelle said, reaching out to rub Lori's arm warmly.

Lori couldn't believe how sweet the woman was being. Comforting her when it should have been the other way around.

"What happened?" Lori asked.

"Well, Meadow, she..." Mrs. Varnelle's voice hitched as she fought to hold back sudden tears. "She vanished. Last night. Without a trace."

"*Vanished?!* Like, she's just gone in the night? Meadow would never. Someone must have..." *Blake.* The name flashed like a giant neon red sign in Lori's mind. If he couldn't get to Lori, attacking Meadow, her best friend, would have been the next best thing in his demented mind. "Did you see anyone around here last night? What time did this happen? Tell me everything. Any detail you can think of, please."

"It was so strange . . . We were sitting there in the living room, me, her, and her dad, we were having our popcorn and family TV time at the end of the night. The popcorn had cayenne pepper on it, which I hated. We were watching . . . *Oh*, what was it? That show with the guy who's very handsome but has that huge chin, *uh* . . . *Brisco County Jr.*! That was it! Anyway, we were watching that, and then suddenly, Meadow says she wants to get some air. I know that she actually wanted to smoke a cigarette, and I don't know why I didn't say anything, but I didn't, and she stepped outside and . . . she never came back."

"What show were you watching?" Lori asked incredulously.

"Brisco County Jr. Why? Is that important?"

Horses' clomping hooves and gunshots from cowboys' revolvers filled Lori's mind. It was the exact show her mother had on the night before. When Blake was at her house. Which meant . . . It couldn't have been Blake. Lori knew he was hovering around her trailer at least until she fell asleep, long after the show had ended.

". . . I don't know why I didn't say anything to her. It was all so quiet, Lori. You think the scariest thing in your life will be loud, big, traumatizing . . . but she was just suddenly, quietly, *gone*," Mrs. Varnelle murmured, more to herself than Lori. Helpless tears welled in the corners of her eyes.

Lori took Mrs. Varnelle's hands in hers and looked the beleaguered woman in the eye. "I'm sorry, Mrs.

Varnelle, but I have to go. I know who did this. I'm going to get Meadow back. I promise you."

Mrs. Varnelle looked both shocked and confused.

She said, "Don't put yourself in danger, sweetie. Just tell the police."

Lori looked about at all the cops surrounding them. The image of that creepy smile flashed in her mind. She shuddered.

"Sorry, Mrs. Varnelle. There's no time to explain, but I don't trust them."

With that, she turned to head back to her vandalized truck. Before she could take a step, Mrs. Varnelle grabbed her by the arm, holding her in place. Lori turned to find her friend's mother sick with worry.

"At least tell me who, Lori. Please. I won't tell the police, I promise."

Lori hesitated. She didn't want to say the name out loud and somehow jinx it, but she couldn't leave Mrs. Varnelle in a state of wondering, paranoid that anyone in town may have taken her daughter.

Lori leaned in close and whispered, "It's Coach Teller."

Chapter 22

Even in the aggressive sunlight of the late spring morning, Coach Teller's home was cold and uninviting. Lori took it in from where she hid in the bushes at the border of his property. The house wasn't that different from Meadow's. A modest brick ranch on a quiet street. Lawn and bushes, neatly trimmed. Plain Jane, suburban America. But knowing who lived there, and who he was keeping captive, lent its vanilla exterior a threatening aura.

There was no sign of life. Curtains pulled tight. No car, though that could have been shut away in the one-car attached garage.

Lori had been crouched in the bushes for nearly ten minutes, trying to figure out the best way to approach while knowing that every second she waited was a second that Teller could be using to do God knows what to her best friend.

The thought made her sick. Furious. Her belly was hot with rage.

But her anger wouldn't get her very far. Her best chance to save Meadow was to take her time and think things through.

Initially, she had intended to simply walk up to his

door and pound away. When he came to the door, she would jump him and ... then what? That was where her plan petered out, and she had to think of something better. Something that would let her get the drop on him.

Creeping on her hands and knees, she moved down the line of bushes running along the front yard. The vegetation ended at a fence surrounding the entirety of Teller's backyard. She kept crawling until she found a small, knotty hole in the pine.

Just before she pressed her eye to the hole, the thought occurred to her that this was how everyone lost an eye in every horror movie ever. *Never peek through the mysterious hole!* With no other idea of how to get a look into what Coach Teller may be doing without revealing herself, she went for it.

Peering through the hole, she saw ... A well-kept back lawn. All was quiet. Nothing stirred on the back deck leading up into the home.

Lori leapt up and gripped the peaked, triangular ends of the fence slats and pulled herself upward, surprised by her own strength. She rose until she was able to get her elbows onto the other side of the fence, and then she hung there, awkwardly, as the wood pressed uncomfortably into her skin. With very little grace, she threw one leg, and then the other, over the top of the fence, careful to avoid the wooden points.

She dropped to the grassy earth below and took her bearings.

Just like from her viewpoint on the other side of the fence, there was nothing. Truly, nothing. Not a lawn chair, or a barbecue, or even a birdfeeder.

"What kind of a psychopath doesn't even have a birdfeeder?" Lori asked herself as she moved stealthily through the grass and up the short flight of stairs leading to the back deck. There, she came face-to-face with a sliding glass door. On the other side of the door were thick fabric curtains that made seeing the interior of the home impossible.

Lori crept toward the door. She knew it would be locked. There was no way Teller would be that careless and she'd be that lucky. No matter. She'd throw herself through the plate glass if she had to. One time, back at a New Year's Eve house party the year before, Ronnie Quail, a burnout kid that Lori was embarrassed to say she'd actually dated for three weeks and two days back in seventh grade, had gotten so stoned that he'd actually walked through a glass door just like this one, thinking it was open. He'd had some minor cuts, but came out all right in the end. If Ronnie Quail could handle it, then Lori knew she could and—

Click.

The door unhitched and slid along the runner when she pulled on it. She couldn't believe her luck. She was in.

She pushed the heavy curtains out of the way and stepped into the living room on high alert, scanning everything before her like Robocop. For a moment, she imagined she actually had power like that, and it gave her a little jolt of confidence.

The home was filled with an eerie quiet. No, more than just quiet. It was a stillness so profound that it felt like another world entirely. A strange planet, where no human had ever set foot.

There were no lights on in the house, and it was hard to make out every detail in the dim light, but, just like the backyard, the inside seemed totally sanitized. Fresh vacuum patterns in the light brown carpet. A maroon sofa and deep green La-Z-Boy, both wrapped in fitted plastic covers. A single painting hung on the far wall of the living room. It featured a ship lost at sea, thrown about on huge, gray-blue waves. A storm roiled above it.

Lori listened for any sign of Meadow or Coach Teller. She could have heard a pin drop on the thick brown carpet. There was only silence.

A trophy case stood against the wall closest to her. She approached, drawn to it for some reason she couldn't quite comprehend. The glass front of the case was perfectly polished with that Windex Streak-Free Shine. The annoying commercial jingle played in Lori's head for a moment, "Streak-free with Ammonia D!," and she wondered if her teacher had been right when she'd suggested Lori had A.D.D. in the third grade.

The glass was so clean and clear that Lori could see her own face mirrored in it as she drew closer. Looking past her reflection, she took in the trophies held within. "Fastest Mile," "Record Javelin Throw," and Gold in a relay race. All track and field medals. None of them extended beyond college. Good as Teller had been, he'd never been able to go pro.

Lori scoffed at him. *What a loser. He couldn't make it out of here, so he doesn't want us to either.*

She didn't hear Coach Teller approach behind her. She had no idea he was there until she saw him reflected in the glass, watching her from the doorway to the kitchen, a crowbar hanging in his hands.

Then he was running at her with a bizarre, herky-jerky gate, like a demented wind-up doll, the glinting steel of the heavy crowbar raised above his head, ready to strike.

Chapter 23

Lori froze as the crowbar sliced through the air and slammed into the plate glass of the trophy case, sending razor-sharp shards through the air. Teller raked the steel through the middle shelf, knocking over trophies and breaking even more glass.

Then the metal bar was rising in the air again, readying itself to be arced down and bashed into Lori's skull.

Finally, the reality of what was happening kicked in. Her survival instinct went into overdrive as she unfroze and spun, screaming at Coach Teller. No words came out, just a primal mix of fear and rage. As she backed away from him, she stumbled over her own feet and landed on the well-maintained brown carpet.

She was reaching for a heavy trophy or an especially large shard of glass, anything to defend herself with, when she heard her name spoken as a shocked question.

"Miss Levi?"

She looked up at Coach Teller to find total shock in his eyes. He still held the crowbar in the air, but was slowly lowering it as his reality caught up to his imagination.

"Miss Levi?" He asked again incredulously. He dropped the crowbar to the floor and struggled to kneel at her side. For the first time, Lori realized that his left leg was in a cast from the ankle to the hip. Hence the strange gait, Lori figured. After an awkward, fumbling moment, the coach settled for leaning over her. He offered her a shaking hand. "I thought you were a burglar. What are you doing in my house? My God, Lori, I could have killed you!"

She regarded him suspiciously for a moment. *If he wanted me dead, he would have done it already.* She took his hand. When she got to her feet, she looked him in the eyes and asked, "Where's Meadow?"

"Meadow? I-I'm so confused right now, and it hurts to stand. Let's sit and talk this through. Can I get you a lemonade?"

"Do you have Diet Pepsi?"

"I don't allow caffeine in this house," he said.

Of course, he didn't. She rolled her eyes but nodded yes, and five minutes later, they were sitting in his bare bones living room. He'd claimed to need to recline in the La-Z-Boy for his leg, so Lori had taken the sofa beneath the giant painting of the ship wreck. Up close, she'd noticed that there were little sailors all falling to their doom from the top deck.

He took a long gulp of his Gatorade and let out a loud *smack*. "So, let's get to the bottom of this. Why are you here? What were you hoping to find?"

"Meadow," Lori said. She sipped from her lemonade and gagged. It was extremely tart. He probably didn't allow sugar in the house either. "I know—*er*, I thought, at least, that you had her here in the house. She's vanished. Someone kidnapped her, and I know it's you who's been—"

"Missing?" he asked, his eyes wide with concern. He leaned forward, then winced in pain and flopped back into the recliner.

"Yeah, she disappeared last night at . . . *uh* . . . I don't know the exact time. Whenever *Brisco County Jr.* was on."

"So between eight and nine o'clock."

". . . sure," she said.

"*Oh no*, this is terrible. I broke my leg yesterday at the end of the school day, around four o'clock. The femur and tibia, just annihilated them. So it couldn't have been me, I was in the hospital until after ten . . . But wait. Why do you think it's me?"

Lori felt the resentment and pain rising in her chest, and she tried to quiet it but couldn't. "Because you *hate* me. You *hate* my band. You hate all of us who are trying to do anything that isn't like ra-ra, crewcut America. You want to ruin us. At first, I thought it was my psycho ex, Blake, but it couldn't have been him because he was too busy stalking me at the time, so I thought it had to be you. I broke in here to save Meadow."

"Hate you? Levi, I don't hate you. I care about you."

"*Ew*, you're like fifty, that's illegal."

"Not like that." Coach Teller rubbed his forehead in frustration and sighed. "I care about you because I see you messing up your life like I did. I was a track and field star back in the day. Really, check the trophies, it's true. I had it all. All-state in high school, and then I got a full-ride scholarship to college. I was really going places. Then I started drinking. Just at parties at first. Then every night. Then I was smoking cigarettes and that sweet Al Green, which tore my lungs up. I came into practice hungover . . . Then I blew it at Nationals my Junior year. They cut me from the team. I didn't even know who I was anymore."

The trophies, thought Lori. *They never went past college. He flamed out.*

"That was it for me. My dreams were over," he said. "I'm extra hard on Crying Lilacs because I see you've got all this talent! I mean, I don't pretend to understand it. It's just horrible noise to me, but I know that people like it, and you're apparently good at it. But Lori, you're just flushing it down the dang commode with the booze and drugs and parties and, jeez, probably sex, which *please* do not share with me if that's going on, I can't stand to hear about it."

Tears began to well in his eyes, and he dabbed clumsily at them with his meaty fists. He took a long pull from the Gatorade, smacked his lips again, and continued.

"You could be a champion if you'd just get in that champion's mindset. So that's why I've been riding you so hard, screaming at you and whatnot, trying to make an example out of you for the other kids to follow. Lord knows I've been going through a rough patch myself with the divorce. Once Destiny left, I just . . . I dunno, maybe I let myself take my frustrations out on you."

Lori shifted uncomfortably on the sofa, and the plastic squeaked out beneath her.

"As you can probably tell, she took darn near everything. Even my birdfeeder. I loved those birds so much . . ."

Eager to get him off the subject of his divorce, Lori asked, "How did you break your leg?"

"I fell fifteen feet off a ladder trying to hang the Battle of the Bands banner up over the auditorium stage."

"*Oh* . . ." Lori said guiltily.

"So . . ." Coach Teller began, then paused to drain the last of his Gatorade. ". . . if you thought I was the one tormenting you kids and that I kidnapped Meadow, then you . . . you thought I *murdered* Memphis? You really think I'd do that?"

Seeing him now, this broken man in his empty house, Lori didn't understand how she could have thought that of him. Then she remembered all the times he'd screamed at her. How he'd threatened to get them pulled from the Battle.

"I don't think you realize how intimidating you can be," Lori said. "You were like, really mean to me, dude."

Coach Teller hung his head. "I know, I-I see that now. I really do. I'm sorry, Lori. I'm sorry it came to all this. If I can help you with Meadow, please let me know how."

Help her? How? She had absolutely no idea who had Meadow now.

The realization that she was back to square one hit Lori hard. Hopelessness flooded into her, filled her.

"Thanks, Coach Teller. But I think I'll just see myself out. Through the front door."

***

With nowhere to be and nowhere to go, Lori drove the old pickup aimlessly around town after leaving Coach Teller's.

Sitting at a red light, Lori thought she might cry, but she couldn't. She was sad, of course, desperately so, but the feeling that roiled within her more than any other was anger.

All that pain and death. And for what? She still didn't know. Why had she and the band been targeted? It didn't make any sense at all.

She wanted to *do* something, but what? She'd tried to help Meadow, and she'd ended up breaking into an innocent person's home and almost getting herself beaten to death with a crowbar. No, she decided, best to leave it to the cops, untrustworthy as they seemed. They were already on it, after all. Maybe they had already tracked Meadow down.

Besides, it wasn't *that* crazy to think that Meadow would have taken off in the night. Maybe to see a boy, maybe to get out of this horrible town and save herself before the killer came for her.

It broke Lori's heart to think that way. She wanted to believe that her best friend would never leave her side, but she had to admit that it was probably the smartest move to get as far away from her as she could. She couldn't blame Meadow.

"Face it, Levi," she said to herself. "It's over. The one good thing in your life is done-zo. Whoever did this has won. The band is dead."

The band is dead. As she finally accepted the idea, a smile crossed her face. Couples in bands were the kiss of death. But, if the band was over, she had nothing to lose. Not that she ever would have given up her dreams for some boy, and talented and cute as he was with killer biceps, Seth was still just a boy.

No, being with Seth was nothing compared to realizing her dream of bringing the Crying Lilacs to MTV, but it was a decent consolation prize.

As she drove around contemplating the possibility, she found herself humming Seth's silly little pop tune, "Beautiful Day." It really was catchy, she decided. The more she hummed it, the more she began to think of ways she could add to it. Finding little flourishes, guitar-driven additions that could make the song a bit more muscular, more punchy. Give it an edge.

Without even realizing it, she had begun to drive back to her mom's trailer to get the Jaguar.

She was a girl with nothing left to lose.

Chapter 24

The Jaguar sat in the passenger seat of the old pickup next to Lori. She'd been so excited to get to Seth's that she hadn't even put it in its case. Just grabbed it from where it lay on her bed and took off with it in the passenger seat.

It made her feel bad to see it sitting there naked and vulnerable, so she strapped it into the seat with the safety belt. At first, it felt a little strange, propped up there like a human. But as she drove on, it seemed like the most natural thing in the world. Like her own little baby was sitting there beside her, safe and sound. Precious cargo.

As she pulled into Seth's neighborhood, it occurred to her that she hadn't really thought through how it would all go down.

Would she babblingly confess her feelings to him? Tell him how hot he was and how much she totally, like, liked him, and how she wanted to get married and sail off into the sunset together? The thought made her cringe.

Maybe it would be casual until it just . . . wasn't. They'd be watching TV together, and they'd both reach for the popcorn bowl together and touch hands, and then, *boom*. Fireworks.

What if she made a move or shared her feelings, and Seth didn't reciprocate? She wondered. What if he told her he felt nothing? That she was gross. To go kick rocks and get out of his face. Seth was too nice to say all that, of course, but still, rejection was rejection. There was no way to make it painless. Sometimes, the bigger the smile, the bigger the hurt.

What if, she thought, a sly grin spreading across her face, *he reciprocated her feelings?* Like, really reciprocated? Would they make out? Would they . . . go all the way?

Lori's face flushed at the thought.

She didn't have much experience with it, despite what everyone in town seemed to think. There had been a few fumbling, awkward times with Blake before she wised up and took off. Then, there were two other guys after. A sweet, but slightly younger guy from a rival band, and then a townie kid after one of their shows that she had picked out as a kind of revenge against Blake, who she'd just broken up with.

At the time they were happening, she'd convinced herself they meant something. Mostly just to give herself the allowance she needed to follow through on her desires.

Maybe this time, if it happened, it really would mean something. The thought pleased her.

Not enough to go through with it right away, probably, but it pleased her nonetheless.

As if coming out of hypnosis, Lori suddenly realized that she was approaching Seth's house. She'd driven all the way through his neighborhood on autopilot, lost in a daydream. She instinctively knew how to get to him.

She pulled the car up into the driveway, feeling the back end of the pickup drop, bump, and scrape against concrete as she took the turn too early and rolled over the curb.

Suddenly, she had the feeling that Seth was watching her. Peering out from one of the top-floor windows with a knowing smile. Like he'd been waiting for her to arrive.

Ugh. She cringed at the thought that he'd seen her take the turn too quickly. *Don't appear so eager.*

As she pulled up, she saw the dark windows of the intimidatingly large house leer down at her. They were all empty. No Seth.

She stopped the pickup at the top of the driveway, pulled the parking brake, and checked her hair in the mirror. A little disheveled, but not bad. She wished she'd stopped and taken a second to primp a bit before leaving. She rooted around in the dash until she found an old scrunchie and pulled her hair back in a ponytail.

Lori hopped out and took a deep breath. After shoving the door roughly closed with her shoulder, she hesitated, then went back into the truck and grabbed the Jaguar. She hoisted it with one hand and trotted up to Seth's front door, feeling like a suitor with a fistful of daisies.

When she got to the front door she hesitated. Was this worth the friendship? Or, forgetting their friendship, their musical partnership? The band may be over, but that didn't mean they might not work together again in another way. After all, she was about to propose that she play lead guitar over "Beautiful Day."

"*Oh*, sack up and go for it!" growled a gruff voice from the depths of her subconscious.

She paced back and forth for a moment. She took a deep breath and counted down . . . One, two, three! Lori rapped her knuckles against the front door. Butterflies flitted about in her stomach as she waited for someone to come to the door.

She was about to knock again when the door slowly creaked open. Only a sliver stood between the door and its frame. Lori peered into it. The house was dim now, not bright and sunny like the first time she'd come over, and it took her eyes a moment to adjust. Finally, she made out the über mom, Mrs. Haggerty, standing behind the door, looking back at her.

"Mrs. Haggerty? Is that you?" Lori asked.

Apparently, it had taken Julie Haggerty a second to see through the sunny glare outside because as soon as she recognized that her visitor was Lori, she threw the door open wide.

"*Oh* my goodness gracious, sweet Lori!" She exclaimed with a big grin. She threw her arms open and waved Lori in for a hug like a giant vulture coming in to land. Normally, Lori would have been put off by the woman's hyperactive positivity, but right now, she was happy to see her. She eagerly stepped up and let Mrs. Haggerty wrap her up in a surprisingly strong hug.

After holding her for a moment, Mrs. Haggerty gently pushed Lori back. She took her face in her hands and looked into her eyes deeply, sweetly.

"Seth told me everything that's been going on, and I am just so, so sorry to hear about this whole awful mess. Poor little Meadow! I cannot imagine who would want to hurt you kids, but it is breaking my heart."

For all of Julie's image-conscious preening, Lori could feel that the woman was being genuine. She really did seem horribly broken up and deeply worried, not just for Seth, but all of them. The point was driven home further for Lori as she examined the woman. Her hair was askew, and she wasn't wearing any makeup at all. Lori actually saw crow's feet creeping about her eyes. She couldn't believe it. Mrs. Haggerty wasn't perfect. She was a human being after all.

"Thank you, Mrs. Haggerty. That really means a lot," Lori said, and she meant it.

"I'm being a terrible hostess! Please come on in."

Julie gestured for Lori to move past her into the house and when she did, she closed the front door behind her with a soft click.

"I know it's awfully dim in here. I apologize. I've got this migraine coming on. I think it's all this fretting. Gotta keep the lights down, if you don't mind."

"No, not at all. I mean, not a problem at all," Lori said. She had never had such a lengthy one-on-one conversation with Mrs. Haggerty, and she was a bit nervous.

She thought Mrs. Haggerty picked up on it, because she then said, "I know you didn't come all this way to see me. Seth is out in the garage doing Lord knows what. You may want to knock before entering."

Julie gave her a wink, but Lori didn't get it and didn't have time to seek an explanation. She did indeed have plans with Seth. She gave Mrs. Haggerty a polite wave and a smile, and moved on through the darkened house toward the garage.

When she made it out there, she found Seth sitting in front of a work table. A small Fender practice amp lay on its face in front of him. The back of the amp was open, and he was fiddling around in its guts, twisting wires. A soldering iron sat heating nearby.

"Seth?" Lori asked, in a voice so quiet, timid even, that it surprised her.

He startled at the sound of her voice and banged his hand against something inside the amp. Wincing, he turned around, an annoyed expression on his face until he saw that it was Lori. Then he broke into a big grin, ignoring the pain.

"Lori, hey! What's up?" he said, rising to meet her. He clocked the Jaguar she held in her hand. He added, "No case? You're playing risky."

"Yeah, I guess I am," she said. She walked to him and laid the guitar gently down on the work table.

"Have they found Meadow?" he asked worriedly.

"No, but the police are on it."

"I'm surprised you're not out there beating the bushes."

"You're right, I should be, I just . . . I came over here because I felt like I wanted to tell you something, but now I'm not sure how to say it or even what it is. It was just this need in me to drive over here and . . . God, Seth, you're right. Meadow's in trouble, I know that, but I don't know what to do and—"

Her voice hitched in her throat, and then his big arms were around her, pulling her close to his muscular chest and holding her tight. No more than a second after he wrapped her in his embrace, did the dam break.

Lori began to sob. She couldn't hold it anymore. All the rage and pain came pouring out of her. Hot tears ran down her cheeks, blackening from her mascara and staining Seth's shirt. Sobs wracked her body, and she shuddered in his arms, then fought against him, humiliated in her vulnerability, momentarily desperate to get out of his grasp, to run from the garage, to get into her truck and drive away to where nobody could find her and see her weakness. She pushed away from him like an animal in a trap, but he held on, gentle yet firm, a cowboy steadying a wild stallion.

Finally, she gave in. She let herself feel safe. She settled her head against his chest and listened to his heart as her weeping slowed to soft whimpers. They stood like that together for some time.

Sniffling, she looked up at him, blinking through a bleary veil of tears. She wanted to tell him how much he meant to her. How she'd been crushing on him since he joined the band. How she was so hungry to kiss him, she felt almost desperate.

Instead, she just did it.

She stepped up on her toes and pressed her lips to his, hard and firm. For a moment, he froze in surprise, then returned the kiss. They melted into each other for a long and passionate moment, months of attraction coming to a sudden head.

Lori had to stifle a small moan as Seth moved his

lips from hers and began to kiss down her neck. Her eyes fluttered as she gave in to his touch, and something caught her eye.

About twenty feet away, on the other side of the garage, hung a shelf. It was cluttered with junk. Cans of wax, spray cleaners, oily rags. Amongst all of it stood the object that had grabbed Lori's attention. A can of spray paint. It was far away and partially obscured by a bottle of high-end leather conditioner, but she could just make out the logo and the color name.

As she read it, she heard Memphis' voice echo in her mind as he identified the exact color used to tag her car on that terrible day . . .

Lawson brand. *Cherry Red*.

Chapter 25

Lori stiffened in Seth's arms. Her kisses went cold. She didn't mean to react. In fact, she kept telling herself not to react. Just make up some excuse, politely remove yourself, and walk out. Heck, smile as you do it and set a date for that night. Then she could hop in her truck and drive away and just disappear. Vanish in a big city somewhere, a place he can never find her.

Seth stepped back and regarded her with a suspicious stare.

"Babe," he said, and the word coming from his lips made her skin crawl. "Babe, what's wrong?"

"*Oh*, nothing, I just got a chill. One of those random things," she lied, and laughed, but she knew from the strange look in his eye that it was already done. She was caught. She had to give it to him. He really could read her well.

Just as well, Lori figured. She knew deep down that no matter where she tried to hide, he wouldn't stop. He would find her. Complete whatever deranged mission he was on. He'd proven that time and again. Besides, if there was even a small chance that Meadow was alive and he had her, maybe even in the very house she was standing in, she couldn't just bail.

She owed it to Meadow to do everything she could to save her, even if it meant risking her life.

Lori backed away from him while keeping a big, cheesy smile plastered on her face. She wished she could make it look normal, natural, but she was so wracked with fear she couldn't, and she knew she looked like Bozo the Clown. He advanced upon with his own creepy, knowing smile.

"A chill? Well, come here, Lori. I'll keep you warm."

She backed into the work table, coming to a sudden stop. Seth and his big, athletic body, which she had been admiring only a moment ago, was blocking her path through the open garage door. She realized, dully, in that lizard part of her brain, that she was trapped.

As if reading her mind, Seth pulled a small plastic box from his pocket. It had a single button on it, which he pressed. With a grinding cry, the garage door chugged to life. It slowly drew closed behind her, casting the garage in near total darkness. The only light came from a small work lamp that Seth had running over his open amp. It cast an eerie, orange glow upon one half of his face, leaving the other side lost in shadow.

He moved within a couple of feet of her. Enough space for him to easily reach out and grab her. To punch her, to throttle her. Just as it looked like he might attack, all of the aggressive tension that had been building in his body slackened. Suddenly, he looked calm and casual. A genuine smile appeared.

"Let's cut the bull, yeah? I don't know how you know all of a sudden, but you know. I can feel it. I know you so, so well, Lori. You can't hide anything from me."

Lori fought through the fear gripping her and regarded him with a stony, fierce gaze. She didn't say a word.

"I need to hear you say it," Seth said.

"Why? That's like, really weird."

"I just do. It's important to me."

"Fine. It was . . . you. The whole time."

Seth let out a little squeak of delight. *"Mmm!* Yummy, yummy, yummy!" He exclaimed. "Thank you so much, babe!"

My god, she thought, *he really is totally psycho.*

"Why?" The word croaked out of her dry throat.

"Why? Goodness, Lori, I . . . Well, I'm really not the one to answer that. That's a question for my better half."

"Is there . . . is there someone else in there with you, Seth? Inside your mind?" Lori asked, remembering a Lifetime Tony Danza movie about multiple personalities that she'd watched late one night on TV with her mom.

Seth opened his mouth to speak, but nothing came out. Instead, he threw his head back and laughed riotously. Long, cackling peels of giggles echoed through the garage.

Before he could collect himself, Lori groped around the work table behind her until she found the Jaguar. She gripped it around its neck and held it up like a baseball bat.

Then she swung. Hard and fast. The body of the guitar caught Seth squarely in the temple.

He dropped to the cement floor like a sack of emotionally unstable potatoes. He lay there, fighting to maintain consciousness, gripping his head and moaning.

Still clutching the Jaguar, Lori turned and maneuvered around the workbench. She sprinted toward the door leading back inside. It seemed insane to be running into the house, but Seth had the garage remote, and it was better than running into the dead end of his studio space. At least in the house, she could hide or find another exit or even find Meadow.

Finding Meadow was all that was on her mind as she burst through the garage door, ran inside, and came face-to-face with the masked killer.

Chapter 26

The masked face stared at her, leering, the breath of its wearer coming hot and hard behind the matte black plastic, sucking wetly at the air.

Lori gasped and backed away as quickly as she could, her butt slamming into the closed door behind her. Already, she could hear Seth on the other side of the door, rattling the knob and pushing desperately to get in. Her weight was the only thing keeping the door shut, and she knew that a few good pushes from Seth, his full body weight thrown against the door, would knock her to the ground.

She put her full weight against the heavy wood and, taking her eye off the masked figure before her for only a moment, she reached down and locked the door with one hand. With the other, she held the Jaguar out in front of her. She tried to draw some confidence, to wield it like a real weapon, but its weight made it droop downward in her one hand, and it felt silly.

He continued to bang away, but the lock held firm.

Satisfied that he was held at bay, she took in the masked figure standing in front of her in the dimly lit hallway.

The usual hooded cape and black clothing was gone. Instead, they wore high-heeled shoes, expensive ones from what Lori could tell. Long, athletic, feminine legs led up to a summery dress that cut just below the knees. It was a bright, floral print. Yellow, with blue iris flowers. The mysterious woman's bare hands and wrists dripped with jewelry. Solid gold. Diamonds. Perfectly manicured French nails. Wavy auburn hair framed the black mask.

It all looked very familiar to Lori . . .

The woman did not move forward. She didn't move at all. Then she spoke, raising her voice to overcome the bangs and grunts from Seth on the other side of the door.

"Seth, sweetie, please stop with the noise. You're making this headache worse," she said, her voice edgy, irritated, but coated in a saccharine sweetness.

Then she took the mask off.

"No way," Lori whispered.

Julie Haggarty, PTA President and Mother of the Year, looked back at her with a mischievous grin. Sweat coated her forehead, pasting locks of hair to her alabaster skin. She took a deep breath and let it out in a long, comically exasperated sigh.

"I tell you, sweetie, I hate wearing this silly old thing. It's just so dang hard to breathe in. And the sweating! Lord Almighty!"

"You, *you, you,*" Lori stammered. She felt as if she might slip into shock, and words were escaping her. Finally, she found them and said, "You're helping him."

"It's nice of you to give Seth the credit of being a mastermind." Her voice carried the distinct edge of derision, a belief that her son wasn't capable of planning a picnic any more than he was a spree of terror and murder. "But in reality, he's helping *me*."

"I-I don't understand. Why?"

"I'd tell you, Lori, but then I'd have to kill you!" Julie's eyes twinkled and her nose wiggled as she laughed at her own little joke. "So, actually, I suppose I can tell you after all. See—"

Bang, bang! Julie was interrupted by Seth throwing himself against the door. The boy had been working at it with such force that the door frame was beginning to splinter around the deadbolt.

"*Oh goodness!* Seth, you stop it now!" Julie hollered. Then, to Lori, she said, "You're gonna want to move away from that door, hon."

Without a thought, Lori did as she was told. As she did, she moved closer to Julie and wondered if she could take on the woman in a physical confrontation. She was older for sure, but very physically fit.

"Don't get any ideas, Lori."

Julie reached down and slipped off her right shoe. Then, without taking her eyes off Lori, she delicately pulled on the tip of the heel. It came away with a little rubberized *pop*, like a cork from a champagne bottle, revealing a savagely sharp steel spike jutting from the shoe. She held it up in a threatening way. Ready to strike if Lori came any closer. Casually, she kicked the other heel off her left foot.

She looked like she was about to say something else to Lori, something venomous, but she was cut off again when Seth leveled a mighty kick to the door. The wood surrounding the lock exploded, sending splinters flying through the air, and the door flew open, slamming into the opposite wall so hard that the knob broke through the drywall and lodged itself there. Seth stood in the doorway, huffing and puffing, sweat pouring down his reddened face. He was seething, his face contorted in anger, his body practically pulsing with rage.

"Seth, you're just tearing the whole dang house up!" Julie scolded.

"Sorry, Mommy," Seth said, his expression immediately mollified, like that of a little boy. He looked down at the carpet, avoiding her withering glare.

Julie turned to Lori and said, "Boys. There's no harder gender to parent. You have to keep them on a very tight leash. Isn't that right, Seth?"

"Yes, Mommy," Seth said to the carpet.

"What the hell is going on here?!" Lori cried out in terror and confusion.

"What do you mean, babe?" Seth asked flatly.

"You've been terrorizing me. You destroyed our instruments, you destroyed everything. You murdered Memphis. Why? You're in the band, Seth! It makes no sense!"

Julie asked, "Lori, do you know what the lyrics to the second verse of your song 'Leave It' are?"

Stunned by the question, Lori couldn't find the words inside her.

Julie answered for her. "It goes something like, 'This town is broken, dead inside / There's nothing here for me / Time for me to take a ride / Leave it all behind, be free.'"

As Julie spoke, the words came back to Lori, locking in. The lyrics were correct, every one of them.

"And the chorus of the song 'Zombie Walk,' how does it go?"

Lori took a breath, let the words come to her. She spoke clearly, confidently. Proud of her work. "Everybody here does the zombie walk / Mindless shuffle, eat, stomp / This whole town does the zombie walk / Praise the Lord with blinders on."

Julie's sly, cruel grin had disappeared. Now her ruby red lips were pulled tight in an angry grimace. Fire burned in her narrowed, snake-like eyes.

"So it's safe to say then, sweetie, that the way you present our lovely little town in your music is . . . negative. Would you agree to that?"

Lori nodded.

"Maybe it's so negative that it's unfair. Cruel. Traitorous."

"I wouldn't agree to that," Lori said.

Julie advanced on her quickly, raising the stiletto, ready to strike like the tail of a scorpion.

"This town gave you everything! They all support your disgusting little band! The kids all dance. The teachers allow you to play at school events. No matter how obscene you behave, they treat you like you're Little Miss Something!"

"That's only because I entertain them!" Lori was shouting now, not realizing that she was doing it until the words escaped her mouth. "Now, because of Nirvana and all these other bands, what I'm doing is cool! Before that, this town treated me like trailer trash, like garbage. I was bullied and talked down to. I did everything I could to fit in, and people still treated me like crap. Now, a few people like my band, and I'm supposed to just forget about all that?

Even now, people like you tell me I'm going to hell! I mean, you murdered one of my best friends to try and keep us down, and you're telling me I should be grateful to this town?!"

For a long moment, Julie was quiet. She sniffed haughtily, nose up in the air. Finally, she said, "So ungrateful. I will not allow your disgusting displays to represent us to the world. It's as simple as that."

"But—but wait—you created the Battle of the Bands? Why?"

"I didn't create it, hon. The offer came to us from the record label, as it came to so many other schools across this great nation. The other PTA members... They liked it. I gently tried to talk them out of it, but they wouldn't stop crowing on about what a great opportunity it was for the children. I couldn't stop it without seeming to be unfair. I must always appear to be impartial, Lori. That's what a good PTA leader does. And I am a *great* PTA leader."

"That's right," Seth interjected, like a church member calling affirmations from the pew.

"I couldn't admit to them that I didn't want to do it because I hated your caterwauling music, your obscene, untrue lyrics. That I hated you, Lori. I hate you. So we held a vote, as all democratic leaders have to allow, and we moved forward with it. But the funny thing is," and then the little grin was playing upon her lips again. "The funny thing is that I realized, suddenly, that they were right. It is a big opportunity for the right young talent."

Seth stepped forward and took his mother by the hand. He gave her an innocent, angelic smile, like a toddler. She squeezed his hand in reply. Lori gagged.

The whole scene made her want to spew all over Julie's clean white carpet.

"My son has been working on his gorgeous songs for years. His vision of the world is sweet and clean. Pure. A proper representation of this town. But everybody is enjoying your filth because of this grunge movement, this Kurt Cobain character. But I knew, if I could get Crying Lilacs out of the way, that he would be a shoe-in to win. Seth and his beautiful music will represent us, our town, on the national stage and show everyone who we really are."

"Who are the people of this town, really?" Lori asked. "Hell, Julie, who are you, deep down?"

"Honey, haven't you been listening?! Me and this town are one and the same! We are the three G's: Good, gracious, and God-fearing."

Seth stepped forward with a proud smile on his face. "Mommy empowered me to join your band. It was all part of the plan. My job was to learn everything I could about you guys. Where you go, what you do. Then use it to destroy you from the inside out."

"So the stupid little masks and capes, you . . . you were both doing it then?"

"The masks aren't stupid!" Seth yelled with a jolt of sudden rage.

Lori didn't flinch and was proud of that.

"Be polite, dear!" Julie slapped her son on the arm. He did flinch. Julie turned her attention back to Lori, smiled, and said, "Yes, that was the two of us working together. It let us both be in two places at once, you see. I had to keep Seth's hands clean and not raise suspicion. Besides, it gave him more time to work on his songs."

Lori looked at her attackers. They were wild-eyed and tense. Ready to pounce. A manic energy radiated from them both. She knew that if she let her guard down for even a second, they would overpower and kill her. She also knew that these two people were more than just unstable. They were angry and emotional and freakishly co-dependent. They would slip up, she knew that. She just needed to keep her cool, find Meadow, and get out of this place.

Meadow.

"What did you do to Meadow?" Lori asked, her voice flinty and cold.

"She's nice and safe," Seth said, thickly. His voice had a husky, creepy quality to it.

He wasn't far away from Lori. If she had a weapon, she could—

Then she remembered that she was still holding her Jaguar. The trusty old Jag. Always there when she needed it. Her dad, her music, was there to protect her.

He was just within range for another nice hit to the temple. As subtly as she could, she began to grip the neck for another swing.

Seth stepped toward her, advancing until he was so close that she could feel his hot breath on her face. It smelled like Barbecue Corn Nuts and Big Red soda. Lori's stomach turned. *How did I miss that when we were kissing?*

"Do you remember, Lori, when we were up on my roof, and you almost fell? You didn't just slip. At least, not by accident. I loosened some of the shingles myself and led you to that spot. The problem is that I chickened out then. I couldn't kill you for real. But Mommy showed me how with the bass string. Now I've had practice. I'm getting really good at it. Now I'm going to do it to you."

A twisted smile played upon Seth's lips. His eyes twinkled. He reached out and ran his index finger along her cheek. She shuddered at his touch, but, despite her fear and revulsion, felt frozen in place, unable to fight, to scream, to run.

Then she felt the power of the Jaguar in her hands. *Screw this creep*. She gripped the neck of the guitar in front of her and jammed it down like a post hole digger, slamming the heavy wood onto Seth's toes. She heard the bones crunch.

He howled in pain and staggered clumsily backward. He tumbled and fell, landing flat on his butt.

Julie raised the stiletto and began to move toward Lori, but she was ready. She swung the guitar outward, catching Julie in the stomach and knocking the wind out of her. Julie doubled over, gasping for breath.

Lori turned on a dime and ran down the hallway, deeper into the Haggertys' house of horrors.

Chapter 27

Lori sprinted down the hall, leading toward the front entrance of the home. The foyer, she knew Julie would have called it. The kitchen and living room blurred past as she ran by. Her lungs burned, and she reminded herself to breathe. She gasped for air and found some slight relief. She was moving down the long, dark hallway with far more speed than she'd had in the mile run. The foyer was in view now.

Coach Teller would be proud of me, she suddenly thought, and almost laughed.

Julie's voice rang out behind her in an enraged, choked cry. "Get her, baby boy! Get her! Get her for Mommy!"

Lori ran into the foyer and whirled around, taking in the space, trying to get her bearings. Sunlight punched through the windows, illuminating the ivory-white tile and enormous cream-colored staircase with its gold accents, creating a gleaming alabaster cage that blinded her for a moment.

Then she found it, blinking through the glary haze: the door. She raced to it and not a moment too soon. Seth had recovered from the attack, and his footsteps were clomping down the hallway, so heavy that they could be heard even on the thick, piled carpet. She noted with relief that he was moving slowly on what were definitely a few broken toes.

Still, he came for her. She knew this time he would kill her.

She pulled on the doorknob. Nothing. She pulled again, harder. It was locked. Panic flooded her as she realized that the door was deadbolted and needed a key to be unlocked.

Seth's shambling footsteps were getting closer. Julie's screaming continued down the hall, now so rage-filled that they were nothing more than incoherent ravings. The cries let Lori know that Julie was still down at the end of the hallway by the garage, where she'd left her. She was incapacitated, at least for the near future. *I must have done a number on her*, Lori thought, proudly. *Maybe broke a rib or two.*

Lori's panicked eyes darted around the room. Before her were the stairs, a dining room off to the right filled with a giant oak table, and, beyond the stairs, another hallway leading off to who knows where. She could risk making her way deeper into the labyrinth of the home, a place that only Seth and Julie knew, or she could follow the path that she remembered. *The roof*, she thought. It was a way out. *Maybe I should shimmy down a drain pipe. Or, heck, jump,* a dark part of her brain suggested. It would be better than giving them the satisfaction of killing her.

First, she had to find Meadow, and if she was still in the house, it seemed a lot more likely that she'd be hidden away in one of the upstairs bedrooms.

Seth's limping gait was growing closer. Without looking down the hall to see where he was, Lori sprinted up the stairs, still carrying the Jaguar. She quickly made it up to the second floor. She paused. To her left and right were two identical hallways, full of rooms. All of them were hidden behind heavy oak doors, shut tight.

Thinking fast, she pulled the scrunchie out of her hair and tossed it down the left hallway. Maybe he was hopped up on enough adrenaline, or was just plain dumb enough to think she'd gone that way and follow.

She took off down the hallway to the right. Past one door, then the next. *Obviously*, she thought, *he'd check those doors first*. Going farther down would buy her more time. Besides, it stood to reason that Meadow would be in a room farther away.

She was at the fourth door down when she heard Seth pounding up the stairs, wincing in pain. She turned the knob, slipped behind the door, and pulled it shut with a soft *click*. Silently, she thanked God for rich people having hinges that didn't squeak.

Then she noticed markings on the other side of the door. Scratch marks. Deep scars in the wood. At first, Lori thought they had come from the nails of an animal. A dog, maybe. But the spacing was too far away. And there were two sets of five markings. She reached down and placed her own hands against the notches in the wood. They matched up perfectly. They were made by human hands.

Lori turned around, and a scream caught in her throat. She was not alone.

Chapter 28

At the far side of the room, positioned in front of a window, sat a hunched figure in a wheelchair. The room was dim, and in the low light, it was difficult to make out any specific features of the person, only that they were slouched and still. The window was blanketed in thick curtains. Whoever it was, they were facing out into nothing . . .

She quickly looked around for a place to hide or escape or even for a weapon that might serve her better than the Jaguar clutched in her shaking hands. But the room was nearly empty. To her left sat an antique, four-poster bed, covered in dust. The bedding was a messy nest of stained, musty sheets. To her right was a large, similarly ancient standing wardrobe. Its doors were covered with cracked mirrors. Unlike the rest of the house, this room had no carpet. It had all been ripped away, leaving only the rough, unfinished wooden slats beneath. Dust motes floated in the air. The whole room smelled musty and sour.

Slowly, the wheelchair began to turn around, its rusty wheels crying out in protest.

Lori pressed her hand against her mouth, desperate to keep the screams in. She knew as bad as whatever this was, Seth finding her would almost certainly be worse.

The wheelchair completed its turn and began to creep slowly toward her. As it drew closer, she was able to make out the figure in the wan light.

It was a man. A young man. He wore nothing but an old terry cloth bathrobe that had once been white but was now stained a sickly yellow. Beneath the robe, which was loosely tied together to cover his groin and thighs, Lori could make out a flash of white. What appeared to be a diaper. The odor in the room called its cleanliness into question.

The young man's skin was deathly pale, his eyes sunken into his face. Once strong, handsome features had been depleted from a lack of sunlight and nourishment. A sheen of sweat coated his forehead. Long, tangled black hair hung around his shoulders, and his face was covered in patchy, wiry black facial hair. His lengthy limbs were as spindly as spider legs.

The young man stopped the chair about ten feet away from Lori. He stared at her with dull eyes and a slack face. Despite his state of decay, something in his eyes, his face, his hair . . . they all seemed somehow familiar to Lori . . .

Seth. He looked like Seth. She was looking at Seth's brother.

Then Lori remembered the urban legends about the Elephant Hole, the story Seth had told her that day, which seemed like a lifetime ago. The sad tale of the boy who leapt into the water and broke his neck. He'd been brain-damaged and paralyzed. And she was looking at him right now.

Lori wondered how she could have not realized it was Seth's brother that she'd heard about all those years. Then she thought about the family's wealth, their power. All those photos with big, important men. They could hide anything they wanted to from the public.

He broke, Lori realized, and Julie couldn't play with him anymore. One of her little boy-dolls had become imperfect in her eyes, an embarrassment, and so she hid him away from everyone, even the rest of the family. Anything Julie found imperfect had to go.

Now he was trapped here, in this home, in this town, forever, Lori thought, horrified at the idea.

Lori pressed her finger against her lips, telling the young man to be quiet.

The young man did nothing. Simply stared at her with dead, vacant eyes.

Then, his hand twitched. Lori stepped back. She watched with a mixture of awe and dread as he slowly raised his left arm into the air. It clearly took extreme effort. As he did so, the sleeve of his robe pulled back a bit, revealing needle punctures, track marks Lori had heard them called, dotting the insides of his forearm. Someone had been shooting him up with drugs. For a long time, too, by the looks of it.

His index finger extended like a hooked talon from his gnarled hand. He was pointing at something. Showing her something. She followed his direction to the wardrobe.

"What . . . What is it? Can I help you?" she whispered.

He said nothing, just held his shaking arm out straight.

Tentatively, Lori walked to the wardrobe. She moved with light steps, carefully not to make a sound and give herself away. Seth was still out there, hunting.

She reached the wardrobe and looked back at the man in the chair. She gave him a look as if to say, "This is what you want, right? For me to open it?"

He said nothing in reply. He only lowered his arm, letting it fall back onto the cracked plastic armrest.

Lori took a deep breath and gripped the burnished bronze handle in her hand. She pulled the door open, and her blood ran cold.

There, slumped inside the wardrobe, was Meadow's lifeless body.

Chapter 29

Lori dropped to her knees beside Meadow. Her friend had duct tape over her mouth, and her feet and wrists were bound with rough rope. Her eyes were closed, and her head drooped down so far that her chin touched her chest. Her body was slack, completely still. Dead weight. Already, tears were welling in Lori's eyes. Lori said, in a whisper heavy with sorrow, "*Oh* no, Meadow! Please no! Please wake up, please!" She gripped her friend's wrist and felt for a pulse. It took her a moment to find it, but it came. Low, so, *so* low, but it was there. Meadow was holding on to life.

"Thank God," Lori said, still crying, her tears having turned to happy ones.

She wanted to shout with joy but knew that Seth was still out there, still searching every room in the house for her. With great care, she took Meadow's face in her hands and turned her so that she could look her friend in the eye. Then she gently shook Meadow by the shoulders and hissed, "Meadow, please wake up."

Meadow did not respond.

Lori gently slapped her face. Finally, Meadow's eyes fluttered open, then fell closed once more.

"Meadow, please," Lori whispered.

Meadow forced her eyes open. Just a crack, but it was enough for Lori. Proof of life. Meadow's voice came soft, muffled beneath the duct tape.

"*Oh*, I'm so sorry," Lori said and gently pulled the tape away.

"W-where am I?" Meadow asked, sounding lost, helpless, in a way that Lori thought her incapable of. She was so spirited and strong.

"You're in Seth's house and you're alive. *Oh*, thank God, you're alive." Lori smoothed her friend's hair out of her face. "Did he hurt you?" she asked, afraid of the answer to come.

"N-no. But Julie stuck a needle in my arm full of some weird stuff. I think it's still in my body 'cause I feel, like, messed up . . ." she murmured and then trailed off.

"I'm going to get you out of here."

Lori went to work desperately trying to untie the binds around Meadow's wrists.

"I don't think I can move that good," Meadow said.

Lori looked back at Seth's brother, who was watching the proceedings. While his eyes still possessed an eerie, vacant look, Lori swore that she could see a small, satisfied smile tugging at the edges of his cracked lips. Regardless of how he felt, Lori knew he would be of no further help. He couldn't have been if he'd wanted to. She went back to focusing on Meadow's bindings, and as she did, she spoke calmly to her friend.

"It's okay if you can't move. I'm going to untie your

hands and—Bingo!" Success. The rope fell free from Meadow's wrists. Lori immediately began working on the ties around her ankles. "I'll leave you here to hide in the wardrobe while I go find a phone. If you do want to make a run for it, don't worry about me. I think Julie is down for the count, but she's probably still downstairs somewhere. The front door is locked, so you'll have to try another. *Oh*, and Seth is hunting me like the Predator out there. He's not looking for you. Maybe that's why he hasn't come in here?"

She pulled the rope free from Meadow's bare ankles and looked with sadness at the red, raw flesh that was left behind. Dropping the rope, she stood and grabbed the Jaguar from where she'd leaned it against the wardrobe.

Meadow regarded the guitar, a vaguely quizzical look in her glassy eyes.

"What's that?" Meadow asked.

Lori knew what she meant. Not what was it literally, but what was it in the context of the hell they were trapped in now.

Lori grinned. "It's my axe."

Meadow gave her a weak smirk in reply and said, "Go get 'em, dude."

Lori gave her a thumbs-up. She began to quietly creep toward the door. As she did, she detoured and stopped in front of Seth's brother—his poor, broken brother, hunched in a rusting wheelchair.

"Thank you," she said, looking down at him.

She felt guilty not kneeling to look him in the eye, but if she was honest with herself, she was too frightened. There was something about him that still made her uneasy. *What was he thinking? Did he have an ulterior motive?* She didn't want to get too close.

He did not respond to her gratitude. She gave him a nod and turned to leave. With surprising quickness, he reached out and gripped her wrist with even more surprising strength.

Lori gasped, but when she looked back down at him, she did not see malice in his eyes. Instead, she saw fear. Desperation. *Please help me*, his eyes said. *Please*.

"I'll get you out of here. I promise."

Then, he did reply. Barely a nod, but it was enough.

Lori pulled her wrist away from his grip. She moved on to the door. There, she knelt and looked beneath the door. The light in the hallway beyond was weak, but she saw no waiting feet. Satisfied, Lori rose and pressed her ear to the door, and listened. She was met with silence. She put her hand on the knob and realized that she didn't know where to go. She had Meadow to think about now. And the brother, she reminded herself.

An image of Seth's see-through phone beside his bed flashed in her mind. His bedroom was up on the third floor . . . There may have been a closer phone, but she couldn't afford to waste time wandering around. Time to hedge her bets. She needed any sure thing she could get. From there, she could crawl out onto the roof and try to signal to a neighbor or some Jet Skiing dingus out on the lake.

This is the smart thing, she told herself. *There's no way this is totally idiotic, and you're going to die.*

She opened the door and stepped out into the hallway.

Chapter 30

As soon as she crept into the hallway, she heard Seth's voice echoing from one of the rooms to Lori's left.

"Don't worry, Mommy, I'll get her!"

She heard no reply from Julie and assured herself that the woman was out of the game, at least for now.

An ominous shadow cast from one of the open bedroom doors. Seth's large body flinging furniture about. Something crashed, and Lori jumped. It sounded to her as if he'd flipped over a desk in his search for her.

He laughed maniacally and called out in a singsong voice, "Come out, come out wherever you are, Lori!"

He's completely lost it, she thought.

To her right were the stairs leading upward. Up to Seth's bedroom. Up to the phone. She bolted in that direction and ran up the stairs. As she went, she heard Seth come out of the bedroom. He was now singing the Beatles' "Hey Jude" off-key in a childlike, high-pitched voice.

She hustled up the last of the stairs and found herself on the smaller landing. Right in front of her was the open door to Seth's bedroom. Standing in the doorway, gazing into the room of a monster, Lori suddenly felt like she was in front of the open jaws of a lion, or something even worse. The most dangerous predator the world had ever known. She imagined herself stepping a single toe over the line into his room and the space itself coming to life and swallowing her whole, dropping her into an endless, horrible void.

"Where are you, you dirty girl?!" Seth's bellowing call cut through the air, jolting her from her waking nightmares. The obvious frustration in his voice gave Lori a fleeting sense of hope. She knew she could do this. She stepped into the monster's mouth and made a beeline for the phone.

When she reached the bedside table, she leaned the Jaguar next to it, keeping it close at hand. As she snatched the phone up, she noticed a framed photo of Julie on the table next to it. It was a glamour shot, soft at the edges. Julie's hair was pulled up in an insane bouffant, and fur lay draped over her shoulders. There was a knowing—no, an *evil* glint in her eyes. Lori shuddered and dialed 911.

The line began to ring. As Lori waited for dispatch to pick up, she looked around the room and realized that it was covered in photos of Julie. Pictures of her winning community awards, leading the PTA, attending local parties and ceremonies. One or two of the photos had Seth in them. None of his father. Certainly none of his brother. Apparently, he'd hidden them away when Lori had come over the first time. Now, the pop star posters were gone, and the whole room was a shrine to the purebred, high-class excellence of Mommy.

"911. What is the nature of your emergency?" The voice croaked through the other end of the line.

"I'm trapped," Lori said, breathlessly. She dove right into it. No time for pleasantries. "I'm being held hostage in the home of Julie Haggerty in Candle Hill."

"Julie Haggerty?" the dispatcher asked. She obviously recognized the name. "As in Julie Haggerty from—"

"All that great stuff? Yeah, that's her. She wants me dead, and her psycho son is gonna do it for her! I need help *now*."

Over the static of the call, Lori could hear Seth dragging his injured foot up the stairs. He would be there in seconds.

"He's coming," she said into the receiver, then set the phone back down in the cradle, ending the call.

Lori placed the phone back on the table, doing her best to match its original place, then grabbed the Jaguar and headed to Seth's window. She breathed a sigh of relief when she discovered that it was already open. She would take luck wherever she could get it. She kicked her leg up and over the sill and ducked out onto the roof.

She stepped to the left side of the window, out of sight. Just in time, too. She heard Seth's childlike voice enter the room behind her.

"*Looooriiii!*"

Lori pressed her back against the wooden siding of the house, feeling its sun-soaked warmth against her skin and trying to draw some kind of reassurance from it. She pulled her knees to her chest and gripped the neck of the Jaguar tight in her sweating fists. She listened as he made his way through the bedroom. He threw open a closet drawer, flipped the mattress off his bed to look between the slats beneath. All of it accompanied by angry grunting, swearing, and a litany of horrible threats against her. Then she heard his steps move toward the window. She heard him hover there. He was so close that she swore she could hear his ragged breathing, smell his sour sweat. She held her breath, desperate not to make a sound.

All it took was for him to stick his head out the window, to take a look to his left, and *BAM*, she was as good as dead.

But he did not stick his head out and look to his left. He swore under his breath and walked away.

Lori broke into a massive grin and gasped for air. She was alive. She'd beaten him. For now. A mix of powerful emotions washed over her all at once. She fought not to dissolve into a fit of laughter right then. On the other hand, she was so happy she felt she just might cry.

Now, she knew, all she had to do was wait for the cops to arrive. She was fantasizing about watching Seth get cuffed and thrown in the back of a cop car when a hand burst through the open window and wrapped itself around her throat.

Chapter 31

Lori immediately began fighting against the grip around her neck. She dropped the Jaguar, which went sliding a few feet away down the gentle slope of the roof, and dug her nails into the muscular forearm jutting from the window. She kicked her feet against the shingles, trying in vain to find purchase so that she could stand and wriggle away.

No matter what she did, though, the hand only tightened around her neck.

Then Seth himself burst through the window and looked at her. His face rocked Lori with equal parts pure shock and fear.

He was wearing a mask, but not the now all-too-familiar black one. No, this one was the same mold, the same featureless face, but it was bone-white. Blood red lipstick was smeared in a crude circle where the mouth would be. Mascara streaked down from the eye holes, as if the mask itself had been sobbing. Topping off the new look was a woman's wig. Aside from being wildly unkempt, the long brown hair was a dead ringer for Julie.

"Jesus Christ, dude!" Lori yelped, or tried to, against the vice grip around her neck.

"You made Mommy sad! You made Mommy cry!" Seth screamed at her.

His words were muffled behind the plastic of the mask, but she could make out his eyes plain as day. They flared so angrily they seemed to actually be on fire, glimmering charcoal embedded in the shadowy eyeholes.

"Screw your mommy, loser!"

Seth, genuinely shocked, gave a dramatic gasp. In that moment, he loosened his grip for a split second.

Pushing with all her might, Lori wrenched his hand away from her throat. She clambered to her feet. Seth's arm flew about, grabbing at the air for her. She stomped on his hand, grinding it down with her heel against the rough roof. Seth yelped in pain.

Careful not to lose her footing, she hustled down the roof and grabbed the Jaguar. She gripped it around the top of its neck and held it aloft in an attack position.

Seth climbed out of the window, revealing he had a weapon of his own. A vicious-looking machete, its honed blade glinting in the afternoon sun. It was no dull weapon like the tools from the barn.

"Come here, Lori. You've been a bad girl. You need to be punished." When he spoke, she could hear the wicked grin beneath his mask.

She knew the Jaguar was no match for the machete. Besides that, he was bigger and stronger than she was. She decided to make the roof her weapon. She would knock him off. This was easier said than done, as she was the one farther down the decline and closer to the edge, and he was still standing near the window. Maybe if she could distract him, throw him off psychologically, she could make him act recklessly. If he let his guard down, he might not notice as she worked the guitar on him to move him toward the edge of the roof.

"Only bad girls kiss boys. You're a bad girl," Seth said as he advanced on her.

"Only bad boys kiss girls," Lori replied through gritted teeth, mimicking him.

"That's not how it works. The rules are different," Seth said with a childish pout.

"Whatever, creep." Lori didn't take her eyes off of him. She stood firm, letting him move down toward her. She could, she thought, use the downward momentum against him. "I met your brother in there. You and your mom really did a number on him."

She expected the line to have some effect on Seth, but he didn't flinch. He just kept moving toward her, his horrible eyes boring into her from behind the mask.

"Your mother . . . She's a real piece of work."

Seth stopped. He cocked his head to the side like a curious spaniel. The tangled nest of brown hair draped over his masked face.

"All her little rules and her dumb accent. The way she played you, man. She made you look like a big baby. Always coming around our shows and yelling like an idiot. But it's all right, she had some good qualities. Like—*oh*, I dunno—she's a mean-spirited witch." Lori gave an exaggerated shrug. "But you know what? I've gotta give you some credit. You really captured her look. Very distinct. Smeared makeup. Messy, 'just got laid' hair. You really captured her bad girl side."

That has to have done it, Lori thought. If that didn't break him, she didn't know what would.

No sooner did the thought pass through her mind than he charged at her, screaming like a banshee, the machete raised in his fist.

As he came for her, she side-stepped and pivoted out of the way. The machete whistled through the air and came down on nothing. Momentum dragged him forward, and he stumbled, nearly fell, and turned back on Lori.

Lori moved around so that she was blocking the direct path back to the window. She had the high ground now.

His wig was falling off, and his mask now sat askew, blocking his vision. He slashed the machete wildly at her, totally disoriented. She swung the Jaguar like an axe and caught his machete hand. The weapon went flying from his hand and skittered across the roof.

"*No!*" he cried out, sounding like a helpless child.

She swung again, and again. With each swipe, he jumped back to avoid being hit. She kept the onslaught coming, working him closer and closer to the edge.

Seth shrieked, "This isn't fair! I hate you, Lori! I hate you!"

She choked up on the neck of the axe and looked him dead in the eye.

"Shut up, mama's boy."

With that, she swung hard. The guitar connected with his jaw, and she heard the sharp crack of bone shattering cut through the air. He cried out and flipped around, stumbled, then fell over the edge of the house.

Chapter 32

"Are you feeling any better, Mead?" Lori asked.

She gingerly pulled the blanket tighter around Meadow. The EMTs had wrapped her up immediately and attached her to a saline drip. Meadow was dehydrated and exhausted, but that had been the extent of her injuries save for the rope burns on her wrists and ankles.

Now they were sitting in the back of an ambulance in the Haggertys' driveway. Four cop cars filled the drive and the street below. Their sirens were off, but their blue and red lights flashed, giving the early afternoon sky around them an otherworldly, candy-coated glow.

Meadow looked at her legs dangling down from the ambulance. She was so short that her feet hung freely in the air.

"I feel like a kid. Like I'm in the high chair at Home Style Buffet again," she said.

Lori tried, but couldn't smile.

"I'm . . . I'm really sorry, Meadow."

Meadow looked at her with surprise and sympathy. "Sorry? Why are you sorry? You saved me. You saved my life, Lori."

"But you never would have been here if it weren't for me. You were right about Seth the whole time. There was something wrong with him, but I just wouldn't see it. Memphis would still be alive. None of this would have happened."

"Lori . . . *Oh*, Lori." Meadow leaned forward and kissed her friend on the forehead. Then she leaned into her, and Lori instinctively put her arm around Meadow's shoulders. "Lori, what did you do wrong? All you did was try to make something cool and get all of us out of here. It's like my dad says sometimes—*uh*, what is it? *Oh*, yeah—You can't be like, blamed for trying. That's what this town does. What all the Julies and Seths of the world do. They blame you for trying. For being yourself. It's messed up."

"I guess you're right. But if I'd pulled the plug before things got crazy, got deadly, then—"

"Stop, dude," Meadow said gently. "We all agreed to keep going, remember? Our band was everything."

Lori nodded. For a long moment, they sat in shared silence, watching the cops scurrying in and out of the house.

"Maybe . . . maybe it still is?" Meadow asked, tentatively testing the waters.

Lori smiled sadly. "I don't think we can replace Memphis."

Meadow snuggled deeper into Lori's embrace. "Maybe we don't have to. I've got an idea."

Lori was about to ask what it was when a bellowing roar sliced through the air and ended the conversation. They looked up to find two EMTs, flanked by cops, carrying a stretcher around the back of the massive house.

Seth was strapped down tight, his neck sandwiched between two big foam blocks. His incoherent yelling was a blend of hateful rage and intense physical agony.

"Where is she?" he shrieked, the words garbled by his broken jaw. "I can't turn my head! Where is that nasty girl? Lori?! Lori, I'm going to kill you!"

As they loaded him into a second ambulance at the end of the driveway, they could hear him singing "Maneater" in a shrill, atonal voice.

Meadow shuddered. "Hall and Oates? I told you he was a poser."

Lori was laughing at the comment when she saw two cops carefully wheeling Seth's brother out of the front door. His malnourished body sat limply in the chair. He was glassy-eyed, dazed. Removed from his reality entirely. But as they wheeled him past their ambulance, he, with great effort, turned and looked at the young women, and Lori was sure that she saw a glint of recognition, gratitude, something profound.

She nodded at him. They wheeled him away, and he vanished into a third and final ambulance. An EMT shut the door, revealing someone standing behind it. The nameless cop.

Lori stiffened with fear as she reminded herself that he was just some weirdo, a fan, actually, for what that was worth. *They had the bad guys. Right?*

He flashed her the same strange, unnerving smile he'd given her at the station, gave a shy little wave, and then disappeared around the back of the ambulance.

"Was that the guy from our benefit show?" Meadow asked, snorting laughter at the absurdity of it.

"Yeah. Just a . . . a fan, I guess. I hope."

"*Oh*, cool," Meadow said absently, then added, "They told me I have to go to the stupid hospital for observation or whatever. You gotta bring me my Melvins tapes. And Mazzy Star. *Oh!* And my Mudhoney one."

"I'll bring you all your tapes, Mead," Lori said, and hugged Meadow tightly.

Detective Threatt passed by, carrying the awful white mask in an evidence bag. It looked like the head of a demented department store mannequin.

"Excuse me Officer, *uh*, Threatt?" Lori asked.

Threatt stopped and, realizing who she was now talking to, tucked the evidence bag behind her so Lori wouldn't have to see the mask. She gave what Lori interpreted to be her attempt at a reassuring smile. Threatt was sporting a new Hawaiian shirt. This one featured little sharks and coconut cocktails. Somehow, her ponytail was even tighter than before.

"It's detective," she said.

"Right."

Lori reached into her back pocket and pulled something out. Her tape recorder. She held it out to the cop.

"I carry this with me everywhere and, well, their confessions are on here. I hit the record button once I realized what was going on. You've got the whole thing right there."

Detective Threatt took it from her with reverent

care. She slipped it into her pocket and said, "I'll take a look at it. You're both very brave, you know?"

"I know," Meadow said. "We're incredible."

Threatt ignored Meadow. She looked to Lori and said, "Looks like I was right about the Cutler kid. Anyway, sorry about the last time we talked. The dog and all that."

Lori was impressed. She hadn't been expecting an apology. But she wasn't ready to get all chummy with Threatt. Not yet. If ever.

She said, "I saw Seth and the other guy, his brother, I think, come out. But where's Julie?"

"We're unable to locate her at this time," Threatt said in her thick drawl.

Lori felt Meadow's arms wrap around her and squeeze as tight as a boa constrictor. Fear flooded her system, turning to ice in her veins.

"What do you mean you can't locate her?" Lori demanded, trying in vain to hold back her frustration and panic.

The cop's face darkened behind her pitch black sunglasses.

"Hate to say it, but she's escaped."

Chapter 33

Wild cheers echoed down the narrow hallway, following Lori and Meadow from the main stage. Both of them were covered in sweat. They had baked under the hot stage lights, and their uniform of ripped jeans and matching black t-shirts hadn't helped. Lori carried her acoustic guitar with her, while Meadow had an acoustic bass.

As it turned out, Meadow's idea that day in the back of the ambulance had been a good one. The two of them didn't replace Memphis on drums. They didn't have a drummer at all. They arranged their songs into acoustic versions. Totally unplugged. The results were simple and yearning, stripped down to the raw feeling that had been behind them the whole time. They even wrote a couple of new tunes together, songs that encompassed what they'd gone through, the shared pain and victory. They'd come through the fire together, and they brought that fire to every word, every note.

The results had been strong. Really strong. They had won the Battle of the Bands at the state level and were catapulted from North Carolina to the national stage, where they had just played a set even more powerful.

Together they raced down the hallway, nearly running with giddy excitement and pounding adrenaline. They passed by the stage manager, who almost dropped his clipboard as he gave them an enthusiastic thumbs up and mouthed the words "Great job!"

They took a hard left and ducked into the greenroom that had the name "Crying Lilacs" printed on it.

"I'll never get over seeing our name on the door," Meadow said dreamily, and threw herself down on the plush, black leather sofa.

Rather carelessly, she leaned the bass against the matching ottoman. Lori eyed it critically.

"*Oh*, gimme a break, it's fine!" Meadow protested, smiling.

Lori laughed and said, "I can't afford to buy you a new one when it breaks."

"You will soon! Money, money, money!" Meadow sang out, and Lori suddenly flashed back to the night behind the bowling alley, when she had sung the same mantra while fanning herself with all of their fundraising cash.

She pushed the image from her mind. No good dwelling on the past, she'd decided. Time to move on. Find a new future. With great care, she set the acoustic guitar in its stand, though even that made her a little nervous.

Telling herself the guitar was safe, she went to the door and locked it. She locked every door of every room she had entered since the day she had walked out of the Haggerty's house.

"Paranoid," Meadow quipped from the sofa.

"Careful," Lori corrected.

She flopped down in one of the tall vanity chairs sitting in front of the makeup mirrors where they had recently spent half an hour telling makeup and hair artists that they didn't want any of that. Meadow, being Meadow, had still done her own makeup, garish and girly. Lori had opted for a completely natural look. The world could take her or leave her as she was.

Still buzzing with excitement from their national debut, Lori turned to Meadow. She was about to speak, but she didn't have to. Meadow could read the question all over her friend's face.

"We fricken' killed it!" she exclaimed.

"We did, didn't we?" Lori asked. Then, "What if we don't win?"

"Lori, we just played live in front of how many people on national TV? Fifty thousand? Fifty billion? If we don't win, I think another label is going to come calling. Besides, do we even want to be on Capitol? Sub Pop is way better. They're like, true."

"What happened to money, money, money?" Lori joked.

"*Aw*, I don't really care about that crap." Meadow waved her hand in the air, as if shooing the very idea away. It was so ridiculous.

"I know, *I know*. Me too. Speaking of, if we don't win . . . does it really matter? The biggest reason I wanted to do this was to show them all that we could. Something for Seth to watch in jail. Something to really piss off Julie, wherever she is."

Seth had spent four months in the hospital, healing

while handcuffed to a bed. Now he was in the county jail, awaiting trial. He hadn't said a word to the press about anything that he and his mother had done. For their part, the local press had done plenty to speculate about the strange relationship between Seth and Julie, and the motives for their bizarre, brutal crimes against Crying Lilacs. Last Lori had heard, he was being kept in solitary confinement because of the high profile of the case.

Sometimes, on late nights, Lori would think of his brother. That poor young man, locked in the prison that his family had made for him. No news had come out about him and Lori imagined that he was fine with that. She liked to think that he was happy and cared for. Living in a home of his own with lots of natural sunlight.

Julie had never been found. Lori checked the papers every day for weeks, but never saw an official update. Locals speculated that she had taken off to some foreign country and was hiding there, incognito, with all of her family's money.

Lori still woke up in the night, certain that the woman was standing over her with a bass string pulled taut in her fists or sharpened drumsticks to plunge into her heart.

"She's gone, man," Meadow reassured her, knowing exactly what Lori was thinking about. They'd had the same conversation many times over the last several months. One of them would get especially scared of Julie's return, and the other would soothe. Then they'd return the favor.

"Right," Lori said.

Don't dwell in the past, she reminded herself, and

again pushed horrible images of Julie from her mind. These thoughts were replaced by a picture of her mother, sitting on the couch in the trailer back home, watching her daughter perform on national television. Had her mom actually watched? Maybe. She knew her dad would have. He would have been disappointed she didn't use the Jaguar they'd built together on her big national debut, but he would have been totally proud nonetheless. She wished so badly that he could have been there for her.

"Say what you will about Julie Haggerty, but at least she came to all of our shows," Lori said absently and snickered. When she saw Meadow's face, she added, "Sorry, I know we're not talking about her. It's been weird playing without the Jaguar, is what I meant, I think."

Meadow sat up and rooted around in a cooler sitting next to the sofa. She came up with a Dr. Pepper and frowned.

"No beer? Come on, man! I'd kill for a PBR." She cracked the soda open and greedily chugged it down regardless. "You'll be back with the old Jag soon. We can't be unplugged forever! You might even have to get around to naming it," she said and belched loudly.

"I think I have a name, actually."

"Yeah? What?"

"Memphis."

Meadow looked up from the soda, excited, nearly spilling Dr. Pepper all over herself. "I love it!" she said with a huge grin.

"And you're right, we'll go back to electric eventually. But we'll need to figure out how to do it without a drummer, I guess."

"Hold that thought. I gotta pee!"

Meadow got up and went to the door leading out into the hallway. Before she could open it, Lori pointed to the small bathroom adjoining their greenroom.

"Just go in there."

"You don't want me to go in there," Meadow said, slapping her belly. "This isn't for private lady bathrooms. This is a public execution."

"*Ugh*, gross!"

Snorting with laughter, Meadow opened the door and walked out into the hallway. The door fell shut behind her and clicked closed. *Unlocked*. Lori fought the immediate urge to jump up and lock it. *Meadow is right*, she told herself. *I am being paranoid. Julie is gone. She's on the run. Vanished to some faraway land.*

You've got to move on sometime.

She let the lock rest.

The guitar, however, sitting in its stand, would not leave her mind. It was expensive, a purchase she made with their fundraising money before they started rehearsals for the acoustic renditions. Yes, it was expensive, and it was safest in its case.

She rose from the vanity chair and picked up the guitar.

"Come on, baby, I'll keep you safe," she said lovingly.

She carried it to the case, knelt, and clumsily undid the latches with one hand. She opened the case and recoiled in terror.

There, painted upon the plush interior of the case's top in brilliant cherry red, was a single phrase.

LOOK BEHIND YOU

ACKNOWLEDGMENTS

Thank you to my wife, JoEllen, for supporting me in all creative endeavors, including this one. Mom and Dad, you're awesome! Gratitude to Caleb J. Pecue, Austin Hinderliter, and the whole Terrorcore crew. You're all amazing. Special thanks to the YA horror greats—R.L. Stine, Christopher Pike, Adam Cesare, Lois Duncan, and so many more. This book wouldn't exist without their work.

ABOUT THE AUTHOR

G.D. Bowlin is the author of *Rock City*, *Deep Dark*, and the forthcoming *Working Man*. A proud member of the Horror Writers Association, he lives in New Jersey with his wife.

www.ingramcontent.com/pod-product-compliance
Lightning Source LLC
LaVergne TN
LVHW030343070526
838199LV00067B/6424